The buildings in Times Square scraped the sky, flashing with huge video billboards that dazzled the zombie nightlife with a flickering digital glow.

A perfect storm of zombie mobs filled the streets, converging on the intersection where Zack and the gang now stood. All around him, Zack saw nothing but a blur of slack-jawed faces and bodies swaying on rubbery legs.

As the undead hordes continued their slow-footed rampage, Zack felt the bass-heavy thump of pop music coming from nearby. The walking corpses began to twitch in unison, closing in on Zack, Madison, Zoe, Ozzie, and Twinkles. The zombies' feet shuffled in step to the beat and their shoulders started to swivel.

The King of Pop's voice taunted them: "And no one's gonna save you from the beasts about to strike!"

Zack felt a kick of panic in his gut—there was no escape from the undead mobs.

THE ZOMBIE CHASERS
EMPIRE STATE OF SLIME

BY JOHN KLOEPFER
ILLUSTRATED BY
DAVID DeGRAND

HARPER
An Imprint of HarperCollinsPublishers

Produced by Alloy Entertainment
151 West 26th Street, New York, NY 10001

Library of Congress Cataloging-in-Publication Data
Kloepfer, John.
    Empire state of slime / by John Kloepfer ; illustrated by
David DeGrand. — First edition.
        pages   cm. — (The zombie chasers ; 4)
    Summary: Six months after the Zombie Chasers discov-
ered the antidote to end the Zombie apocalypse, Zack Clarke
and friends discover, during a class trip to New York City,
that the living dead may not be gone for good.
    ISBN 978-0-06-223096-6
    [1. Zombies—Fiction.   2. Survival—Fiction.   3. New
York (N.Y.)—Fiction.   4. Humorous stories.]   I. DeGrand,
David, illustrator.   II. Title.
PZ7.K8646Emp   2013   2013012100
[Fic]—dc23   CIP
                                                 AC

14 15 16 17 CG/OPM 10 9 8 7 6 5 4 3
❖
First paperback edition, 2014

Staten Island Ferry

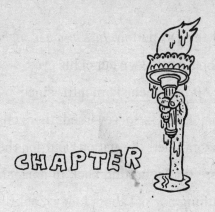

CHAPTER 1

A chill shivered up Zack Clarke's legs as he walked barefoot down his deserted street, casting a nervous glance over his shoulder. Suddenly the shadows warped off the lawn and morphed into undead flesh-and-blood figures. Mom and Dad, Rice and Ozzie, Zoe and Madison, and even Twinkles surrounded Zack on all sides, snarling at him through jagged zombie teeth, hungry for brains.

"Ack!" Zack yelled, and started to run.

Beep-beep-beep!

Zack shot straight up in bed, his heart racing. The hotel alarm clock blared in his ear. He reached over and hit the Off button. *Just another nightmare*, he thought, rubbing the sleep out of his eyes.

It had been six months since Zack, Rice, Madison, Zoe, and Ozzie reversed the zombie outbreak and unzombified the nation, and for the most part things were finally getting back to normal. Except there was nothing normal about today. Zack and his friends were about to appear on the *Good Morning Show* for the opening of the new zombie exhibit at the Museum of Natural History.

Zack looked around the hotel room, bleary-eyed. The television was on and Rice sat on the end of his bed, spooning a bowl of cereal into his mouth, hypnotized by an ancient Tom and Jerry cartoon.

"What's going on?" Zack asked, looking over at Ozzie's cot, which was neatly made with a folded stack of green camouflage T-shirts on the end. "Where's Ozzie?"

"He's already on set. He went with Madison and Zoe, like, twenty minutes ago." Rice looked at the clock and turned to Zack. "You'd better get moving, man. Our car's gonna be here in fifteen minutes."

2

Zack grumbled something under his breath, threw off the covers, then walked sluggishly to the bathroom and slammed the door. He had never been much of a morning person.

The boys rode the elevator down and walked through the lobby out to the street, where a limo driver stood holding a sign: CLARKE & RICE.

The driver opened the door, and the boys hopped in, sinking down into the cushy leather seats. The limo pulled away from the curb and merged into the honking New York City rush hour.

"Yo," Rice said. "How sweet is it that we get to be on TV?"

"Pretty sweet, I guess." Zack shrugged. "I don't know. Did they have to schedule the interview during our school trip to New York City? Almost the entire seventh and eighth grades are going to be there, watching us."

"Exactly!" Rice said. "It's your chance to show off some of that Zack Clarke charm I keep telling the Fearsome Foursome about." The Fearsome Foursome was a clique of the four most popular girls in seventh grade. Gabby Kahn, Jamie Joran, Mandy Pitman, and Ayana Healy made up the ruthless crew of mini mean girls, and they were a force to be reckoned with.

"Yeah, about them," Zack said. "Not interested."

"But we're national heroes now, dude. The old rules don't apply to us anymore," Rice said. "Do you know what hanging out with the Fearsome Foursome could

do for our street cred? Not to mention, I heard from a fairly reliable source that last week during gym class Gabby said she kind of likes y—"

"Rice!" Zack shushed his friend, pointing to the driver's eyes peeking back at them in the rearview mirror. "Dude, we have bigger things to focus on right now," Zack said. "Like not sounding stupid on live television. Or screwing up the museum exhibit opening."

Zack got nervous just giving a presentation in school, and now he was supposed to do a live interview in front of millions of people? Right after the outbreak, Zack and the gang had given a few local interviews back in Arizona, but this was different. This was the big time. He took a deep breath and exhaled slowly, gazing out the window at the crisp blue New York morning.

The city blocks flew by, and before long the car pulled over to the curb.

"Here you go, fellas," said the driver. "The Museum of Natural History."

Rice peered over his flashy prescription sunglasses, glanced out the window, and frowned. "What's this? Where's the paparazzi? The red carpet?"

"Real funny, kid," the driver said. "Now scram."

Zack and Rice hopped out of the car. Next to Zack, Rice stood out in shiny black jeans, brand-new high-tops, and a gold chain around his neck. He sported a warm-up jacket over a freshly ironed T-shirt with a red slash X-ing out a BurgerDog logo on the front. The whole out-fit looked like something out of a rap video.

"You look insane," Zack said, smirking at his pal.

"Don't hate the player, Zacky," Rice said, popping his collar. "Hate the game." Rice adjusted his sunglasses and swaggered off.

At the top of the steps, two cameras on tall black tripods faced the front of the museum. Over the entrance hung a large banner that read: NECROINFECTIOUS GENETIC PANDEMIC!

Zack and Rice walked around the camera setup and found Madison and Zoe sitting under the makeup tent in director-style chairs, getting preshow manicures.

"Looking good, ladies!" Rice said, stepping inside. He flexed his muscles in the full-length mirror.

Zoe laughed out loud. "Rice, stop it. You're so not diesel."

Rice ignored Zoe's comment. "Nice outfit, Madison," he said, admiring her spring dress and matching high-heeled shoes.

"Thanks, Ricey-poo," Madison said, puckering

her lips at her own reflection. "You don't look so bad yourself."

"Not so sure I can say the same for you, little bro," Zoe said, looking her brother up and down.

Zack glanced down at his plain white shirt and black dress pants. "What's wrong with this?"

"Ouch!" Madison let out a high-pitched yelp. "You cut me!" she said, pulling her hand back and glowering at the manicurist.

"Well, don't just stand there like an imbecile," Zoe shouted, pronouncing the last syllable *seal*. "Go get her a Band-Aid! Now!" She ordered the makeup girl away but kept her eyes on Zack. "You're going on national television representing your school, your family, and, most important, me, so you can't be dressing like some lame-o. Madison, can you please back me up?"

Madison pinched her cut finger and inspected Zack's wardrobe choice. "Ee-you," she said. "No offense, Zack, but it's totally boring!"

Zack looked Rice dead in the eye. "Dude, why didn't

you tell me my clothes looked totally boring back at the hotel?"

"Don't listen to these two," said Rice. "We have to go to wardrobe anyway, so we'll have time to give you a quick makeover."

Zack shuddered at the thought. No thanks to his sister and Madison, he had developed a slight phobia of people trying to make him look pretty.

Rice put his arm around Zack's shoulders and gave him a squeeze. "Don't worry, buddy . . . no girls allowed this time."

They found their way to the wardrobe trailer across the street on Central Park West, but as Zack reached for the door, it flew open in his face.

Wham!

The door kicker struck a rigid pose and made a long, high-pitched shriek like a martial-arts master in a kung fu flick.

Ozzie Briggs stood in the doorframe wearing a white karate *gi* with a black belt cinched around his waist.

"Nice kick, Oz!" Rice said, in awe of his pal.

"What's up, Ozzie?" Zack said, slapping him five. "You scared the crud out of me."

"Sorry, man. Just getting warmed up for my little demonstration," Ozzie replied, tightening his belt. "I've got to get ready backstage, guys. Check you on the flip side." He grabbed his nunchakus and exited the trailer.

A few minutes later Zack emerged from the dressing room in a pair of skinny blue jeans and a hip-looking button-down with extra buttons and pockets to make it look extra cool. According to Rice, there was a direct correlation between something's coolness and the amount of pockets, loops, buttons, and straps it had. Zack checked himself out in the full-length mirror. Rice wasn't such a bad stylist after all.

As the boys stepped out of the trailer, some guy with a headpiece and microphone walked up to them and said, "Two-minute warning. They need you on standby."

As Zack and Rice followed the TV guy up the museum steps, they looked down and saw a mass of people assembled outside the red velvet ropes. In the crowd, three tween girls held up signs for each of the boys.

I LOVE YOU, ZC!

RICE, WILL YOU MARRY ME?

CALL ME, OZZIE! 867-5309—JENNY.

Rice blew a little smooch to the girl holding up the marriage proposal, and she fainted into the arms of her two friends. Zack crinkled his eyebrows and kept moving, trying to ignore them. Another crew member rushed Zack and Rice to their spots next to Madison and Zoe.

Zack felt the butterflies fluttering in his belly.

"Five . . . four . . . three . . . two . . . one!" The cameras were rolling and they were live.

The host turned and spoke directly to the camera.

"Six months ago our world was turned into a nightmare of undead carnage. The whole country was on the brink of annihilation. And if not for the efforts of a few middle schoolers from Phoenix, Arizona, we all might still be zombified. Please welcome Zack and Zoe Clarke, Johnston Rice, and the one, the only Madison Miller." The audience applauded as the four of them waved to the cheering crowd.

Madison leaned over and grabbed the microphone from the host. "Don't forget about Twinkles," she said, and pulled the little Boggle puppy from her purse.

"How could I have forgotten Twinkles?" The host smiled at Madison and continued. "Together these unlikely heroes transported the zombie antidote across the country to BurgerDog CEO and famed geneticist Thaddeus Duplessis, who helped them mass-produce the brain-flavored unzombifying popcorn antidote." The TV host turned to them. "What were you all feeling when you confronted the person to blame for this utter catastrophe?"

"Honestly," Zoe piped up first, "I really wanted to make him pay for what he did. I mean, he was totally

responsible for zombifying this." She waved her hand in front of her face.

"Tragic." The host nodded thoughtfully, shuffling her note cards. "The next question is for Madison: What was going through your mind when you realized America's only hope for survival was you?"

"Um, it was pretty intense," Madison said. "I mean, I was happy to do it. But once we made all that popcorn, it was nice to get a break from being the antidote." She paused, flipping her hair to the side. "All I really know is, there's no way I'd even be here right now if it weren't for these guys watching my back."

"And neither would any of us," said the host, and the crowd cheered. "Zack, how about you? What was it like to hold the fate of the world in your hands?"

"Well," said Zack, "it was scary, and there wasn't a lot of time to think about what to do next. We just kind of reacted and went with our instincts and—"

"Yeah," Rice cut him off. "Take me, for instance. Like, one day I'm watching zombies get their butts kicked in some movie—can I say 'butt' on TV?"

"Uh-huh." The host nodded yes, and Rice continued.

"And then the next day, I'm out there chasing actual zombies with my friends. It was awesome!"

"So, Rice," said the host as she cleared her throat. "Tell us what you've been up to now that your zombie-chasing days are over."

"Actually," Rice said coyly, "I'm workshopping a musical comedy I wrote over the winter. It's a Shakespearean hip-hopera entitled *Much Ado about Yo Mama*."

The host cracked a smile. "That sounds wonderful, Rice. Now, everyone, please welcome Oswald Briggs!"

The crowd clapped, but Ozzie was nowhere in sight. The cameraman panned across the platform. Then, as the camera swung back, Ozzie catapulted out from behind a pillar into a long series of backflip handsprings. He landed in crouching-tiger position, alert, gripping his nunchaku, ready for battle.

The crowd gasped involuntarily and then cheered.

All of a sudden a band of zombie stuntmen appeared from behind two curtained-off areas of the stage and staggered toward Ozzie.

"Blargghlesgargles!" moaned the undead phonies.

The crowd gasped again. With a combination of kicks, jabs, flips, and elbow chops, Ozzie took down the band of "undead" stuntmen one by one. He did a flying gymnastic cartwheel round-off combo to finish the routine, leaving the entire zombie stunt team conked out on the floor.

The audience erupted as Ozzie took a bow and then trotted over to join his friends for the rest of the interview.

"Ozzie," the host said, "you are obviously a talented martial artist, but what are you doing now that you're done saving the world from legions of the undead?"

"Well," Ozzie began, "after me and my dad moved to Phoenix and I started school with these guys, my dad and I created a charity with Rice's dad, who makes prosthetic robotic limbs

for a living. The charity sponsors people who lost an arm or a leg during the BurgerDog outbreak, but can't afford the procedure. So far we've supplied over one thousand less fortunate people with new limbs."

"Give it up for the Zombie Chasers, everyone. America's heroes!" the host said. "And now, we are proud to have a very special guest. Please welcome the mayor of New York City!"

The mayor sauntered onstage, leaned over the podium, and spoke into the microphone. "On behalf of the five boroughs, I present to you exceptional young men and women the key to the city of New York. Thank you for your fine display of teamwork and perseverance in our country's desperate time of need."

Zack walked over first and shook the mayor's hand. Then all five of them posed for a picture and accepted their keys to the city.

With the crowd cheering, Madison snipped the ribbon hung across the entrance, and the museum doors opened.

Zack took a long deep breath and sighed, thankful that the hard part of the trip was over.

CHAPTER 2

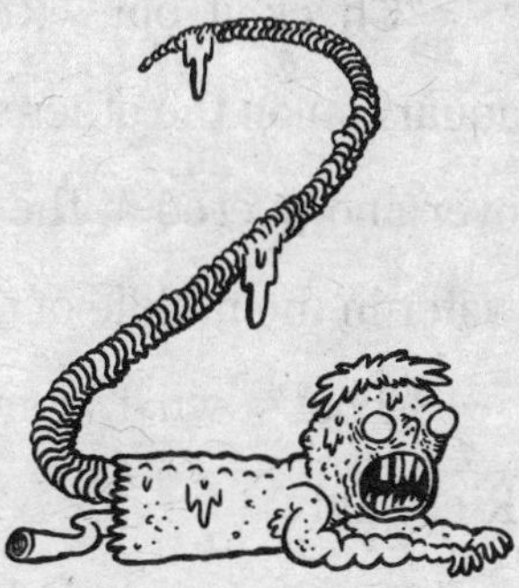

Zack, Rice, and Ozzie strolled through the high-ceilinged foyer of the museum. A few feet inside the exhibit stood three life-size wax statues illustrating the different stages of zombie decomposition. The third and most grotesque zombie replica slouched with a hunch in the shoulders, its arms drooping below the knee. Large areas of skin were melted away, revealing slick, glossy patches of red meat beneath the flesh. Farther down, a massive stuffed zombie cow-pig from the BurgerDog cattle ranch stared down on them from a large pedestal, with a placard that read: BOVINE HOG. It was almost more revolting now than when it was alive.

"Check it out," Rice said, pointing toward a big aquarium on the other side of the room. The boys raced over and peered at the live jellyfish specimen treading water in the middle of the tank.

"That's what zombified the BurgerDog virus," Rice said.

"Come on, dork brains," Madison said, strolling through the museum gallery. "They're about to show a movie about us."

"Yes," Zoe said in a motherly tone. "There will be plenty of time to be complete losers later on."

The girls skipped off and vanished to the front of the line gathering outside the screening room.

A few minutes later, the boys took their reserved seats in front. The theater was a blank white room equipped with a projector and a few rows of seats on each side.

The lights dimmed and the screen lit up.

The documentary began with a series of clips from the news footage during the outbreak, followed by a brief history of Thaddeus Duplessis, the creator of BurgerDog. Next there were interviews with their parents, Colonel Briggs, Greg Bansal-Jones, Sergeant Patrick, and Private Michaels. There was also authentic security camera footage from their trek across the country, their pit stop at the Mall of America, and their journey to the BurgerDog cattle ranch way out in Montana.

All of a sudden the projector cut out and another scene interrupted the documentary.

Zack watched in disbelief as black-and-white spy-cam footage of his bedroom flashed on the big screen, and a techno dance beat thumped in the background.

Zack knew the song immediately. It was his favorite song to geek out to when he was alone in his room. Zack jumped into the frame wearing a white T-shirt and plaid pajama pants before trying out a series of embarrassing dance moves in front of the mirror.

The audience started to laugh. Zack turned around and looked behind him. The Fearsome Foursome giggled in the back row. Above them, Zack caught a glimpse of two silhouettes up in the projection booth: Madison and Zoe, doubled over with laughter. When they saw Zack watching them, they both smiled at him and gave a little wave.

Rice looked at Zack. "You want to get them back for this?"

Zack took a deep breath. "Absolutely."

"Good," said Rice. "I've got just the thing. We have to wait until the timing is perfect, though." He patted the contents of his trusty backpack and the documentary came back on.

The film concluded with a newsreel chronicle of Operation: Scatterbrains where dozens of fire planes

dumped loads of brain-flavored, antidote-covered popcorn across the continent. As the lights turned back on,
the crowd applauded. Some of his classmates were still
snickering, but Zack couldn't help but smile. They had
saved the world—no matter how many times his sister
could embarrass him—and that never stopped being
the coolest thing ever.

Shortly after the museum opening, the seventh- and
eighth-grade classes of Romero Middle School gathered
in Central Park for lunch. They all laid out picnic blan-
kets, waiting for the pizza to arrive.

Madison and Zoe were lying out on their blanket,
catching some rays. They had their sleeves rolled up
and their sunglasses on. Next to them Zack, Rice, and
Ozzie sat on a blanket of their own, people-watching in
the shade. All types of folks populated the park: joggers,
cyclists, Frisbee throwers, businesspeople, and tourists
basked in the fine spring day.

"Look at all these people . . . ," said Ozzie as he pointed to a bunch of New Yorkers strolling through the park. "What a freak show!"

He stared at a man teetering through the park on stilts. Even more bizarre was the stilt walker's getup—he was dressed like a circus clown, with an orange Afro wig, bright red nose, white face paint, polka-dotted pants, a poofy shirt, and purple suspenders.

It was strange to see all of these weirdos in broad daylight. Back home in Phoenix, the freaks usually came out only after dark.

Just then Zack saw Rice's eyes shift surreptitiously from side to side. "Here we go, boys." Rice extracted a small black device with a speaker from his backpack. He crawled forward toward Madison and Zoe, reached his hand under their picnic blanket, and planted the gadget there, unnoticed by the sunbathing girls.

"What the heck was that thing?" Zack and Ozzie both asked at the same time when Rice returned.

"That, my friends," said Rice, "is a state-of-the-art, remote-controlled noisemaker." He held up the tiny remote. "With the click of a button, that little gizmo under there will mimic the sound of any bodily function a human being has to offer. It's like a whoopee cushion, except way awesomer."

"Sick," Zack said, and looked away, trying to ignore his older sis for fear he might give Rice's plan away. Over his shoulder he spotted a guy in a red polo shirt and cap walking toward them. He was balancing a dozen pizza boxes on his upturned palms. "Hey, pizza guy's here!"

"Okay, everybody line up," said their Spanish teacher, Mrs. Gonzalez. "Only two slices per person, please!"

As all the hungry middle schoolers raced to form a line, Madison stood in front of their music and drama teacher, Ms. Merriweather. "Excuse me, Ms. M," said Madison. "I need another Band-Aid. This one's getting all grody." She peeled off her old Band-Aid and tossed it into the trash can.

"Hold on one second," Ms. Merriweather said, turning to Madison. "Oh, my gosh." She slapped her forehead. "Honey, I'm so sorry; I forgot to order you a personal vegan pie."

"But," Madison said, whimpering a little, "I'm, like, totally famished, Ms. M. . . ."

The delivery guy scratched his head. "I don't think we have vegan anything."

"That's okay," Madison said, making a pouty face. "I'll just pick off the cheese, I guess."

After everyone got their pizza, Zack sat back down on the picnic blanket between Ozzie and Rice. He folded his pepperoni slice in half and took a monster bite. The pizza was the best he'd ever tasted, Zack thought, as he polished off the slice.

"This is the life . . . real New York City pizza," Rice

said, airplaning a stray pepperoni into his mouth.

Zack glanced over at his sister, who was talking to Madison with her mouth full of pizza crust. They were both giggling as they watched two college-age boys playing catch with a football. Madison grabbed another slice of pizza, peeled the cheese off and started to scarf it down.

"Well, what are we waiting for?" Ozzie whisper-yelled. "Let's try this thing out!"

Rice pressed one of the remote-control buttons with his thumb, and a series of hideous fart noises erupted from underneath the girls' blanket. Zoe and Madison both sat up and lifted their sunglasses. "Ew, dude," Zoe said. "Gross."

"Uh-uh." Madison laughed. "That wasn't me."

"Twinkles?" The girls jinxed each other.

Twinkles barked defensively. "Arf-arf!"

Zack and Ozzie covered their mouths, cracking up silently.

Rice pressed the remote control again and a louder

barrage of grotesque bodily sounds reverberated from underneath the girls. Heads began to turn toward Madison and Zoe.

"What are you freaks looking at?" Zoe yelled at the class. "It's not us!"

"Yeah," Madison said. "Stop looking at us. It's totally rude!"

Rice hit the button one more time and another foul-sounding noise erupted, causing the entire class to burst into a fit of laughter. Just then an adult-size silhouette appeared, casting a shadow on Rice's moment in the sun.

"Arroz!" Mrs. Gonzalez stood towering over them. *"Dámelo.* Give it to me."

Rice glanced up at their Spanish teacher, gave her his best aw-shucks face, and then passed her the remote control.

Zoe stood up and walked over. "Thanks, Mrs. G," she said, handing their chaperone the other half of the mischievous gadget, shaking her head. "Kids today." Zoe then turned to the boys as their teacher walked away. "I'm glad you three had your little fun." She scowled. "Because for the rest of this trip you all better sleep with one eye open."

"Yeah, yeah, Zoe," Ozzie said under his breath as Zoe turned away. "We're real scared."

"Okay, everyone!" Ms. Merriweather raised her voice above all their conversations. "Please throw away your plates and form a single-file line over there." She pointed to the black entry gate leading in and out of the park, where two bright red double-decker tour buses had just pulled up to the curb.

"I call front seat on the top level!" yelled Zack as he dumped his trash and took off running.

"Last one there is a rotten zombie!" Rice's voice trailed off as they hustled for the buses.

CHAPTER 3

Zack, Rice, and Ozzie peered off the observation deck at the top of the Empire State Building as the sun lowered on the horizon. The sky blazed bright red-orange with streaks of pink clouds. The boys gazed out across the panoramic view of the big city. From the hundred and second floor of the sky-scraper, the New Yorkers below looked tinier than ants, more like the size of ticks, hustling and bustling by the thousands upon thousands all over the concrete island of Manhattan.

"Check it out," Ozzie said, pointing south toward Liberty Island. "That's where we just were."

From that height they could see all the places they had gone throughout the day. First they had visited Ellis Island and the Statue of Liberty, the 9/11 Memorial, then up through SoHo and over to Greenwich Village. While the girls had gone shopping, the boys stopped at a street food cart and had a contest to see who could eat the most falafel balls. Rice won that contest hands down, with Zack coming in a close second.

It was a pretty fun trip, but Zack was dying to get back to the hotel. His feet were killing him.

Ms. Merriweather looked at her watch and raised her hand, getting everyone's attention. "Everybody line up!"

Zack jumped in line behind Madison, and the students began to shuffle back inside single-file.

"Psst!" Rice grabbed Zack by the shirt collar and yanked him around the corner of the observation deck. They waited there until the coast was clear.

"What the heck, man?" Zack said, massaging his neck. "That's gonna leave a mark." Rice ignored him, dropping to one knee and opening up his trusty backpack. "Dude, what are you doing?" asked Zack.

"I'm going to reenact the finale scene from *King Kong* real quick. . . ." Rice rummaged around in his pack and produced a gorilla mask, a Barbie doll, and a model airplane strung to a wooden stick.

"Fine. Just hurry up." Zack chuckled to himself. "I don't want to get in trouble with Mrs. G." Zack took Rice's smartphone and clicked the camera icon.

"Okay," Rice said, pulling the mask over his head. "Let's do this." He stood in front of the New York skyline and began to make some startlingly realistic monkey noises. In one hand he held the Barbie; in the other, he dangled the model airplane strung to the stick so that it dive-bombed in front of his face.

Zack clicked a few different pictures and then scrolled through them. "I think we got it," he said. "Can we go now?"

Rice took off the King Kong mask. He was sweating bullets. "Whew! This thing is hot as heck!" He took a deep breath and exhaled slowly.

"You okay, man?" Zack pocketed the smartphone

and raised an eyebrow at his friend. "You don't look so great."

"Yeah, yeah, yeah, I'm good. I'm good. . . ."

Then, all of a sudden, Rice fell to his knees and flopped to one side on the ground. He clutched his stomach and let out a painful groan, coughing and squawking as a wave of spasms rippled through his spine.

"Dude, give it a rest!" Zack said. "I told you, like, three months ago I'm not falling for any more of your stupid zombie fakeouts."

Down on the ground, Rice clutched his throat and gagged melodramatically before his body went completely limp. His head lolled to the side, and his tongue hung out of his mouth.

"I swear, if you're messing with me . . ."

Zack knelt down next to Rice. Something was wrong. He grabbed Rice's wrist but couldn't find his pulse. Rice wasn't breathing either! Zack's heart started beating wildly as his best friend's slumped body started to wriggle and convulse again uncontrollably.

"Somebody help!" Zack called out. But no one heard him. They were all alone out on the observation deck. He laid his friend's head down on the ground and ran for the door. Behind him Rice shot up with a jolt, growling like a zombie.

Zack spun around as the boy who cried zombie hauled himself up and wobbled in place with his arms out in front of him. "Ha ha, real funny!" Zack shouted. But this was no joke.

Rice's face was twisted in a horrible grimace. His eyes were dull and pallid, and his complexion was rapidly turning a grayish green. The veins around his eyes spiderwebbed suddenly, as if they had been pumped full of dark green ink. Rice's left eye was focused slightly off center, while the right eyeball looked directly at Zack.

Zombie Rice hobbled across the deck and launched himself at Zack. *"Blaaargh!"*

"Dude!" Zack screamed, backing away quickly. "Chill!"

Rice lunged at Zack again, screeching like a savage hyena. He swiped his arms wildly, his hands whizzing by an inch in front of Zack's nose.

Zack backpedaled and tripped on an orange-and-white cone, falling back into a sectioned-off corner of the deck where the guardrail was undergoing construction. Zombie Rice kept after him,

thrashing through the construction area. He waddled slowly forward with twin fangs of saliva drooling from his mouth. Zack reached over quickly and picked up a metal pipe, then hopped to his feet and raised it defensively. "Rice, if you don't stop trying to eat my brains, I will be forced to hit you with this really freaking hard. Do you understand?"

Rice sneered at Zack with a blank-eyed stare and a mischievous half smile. *"Gibble-gabble-glarghle!"* he blabbered, and charged forward once again.

Zack raised the pipe like a batter bunting a fastball and deflected his rezombified friend's attack, sending Rice flying into the broken guardrail.

"Rice!" Zack called, rushing to the spot as his best friend flipped clean over the side of the Empire State Building. Peering over the ledge, Zack gasped in horror. The steel bars creaked as zombie Rice dangled one hundred and two stories above the ground, hanging with both hands from the bent metal guardrail.

Zack felt a surge of panic rushing through his chest and stretched his arm as far as it would go. "Come on, buddy," he urged, finally coiling his fingers around Rice's wrist.

Zombie Rice abandoned the guardrail and instead grabbed Zack's forearm with both zombified hands. Zack strained with every ounce of strength he had, but he couldn't lift Rice to save his life. Zack didn't know how much longer he could hold on.

"Ow, dude!" Zack yelled, almost losing his grip as zombie Rice gnawed at Zack's finger joints. "No, no, no! Bad zombie!" He grimaced, tightening his grasp despite the pain of being Rice's knuckle sandwich.

"Here, Rice," Zack said, bowing his head. "I got brains, right here . . . all you can eat! Come and get 'em."

Immediately, Zack's voice caught his undead friend's attention, and with his newfound target in sight, zombie Rice scaled the side of the building using Zack's arm for leverage and his delicious brain-filled cranium as motivation. As Rice reached the top, Zack gave one final heave, pulling with all his might. Rice tumbled over the ledge and landed face-first on top of the observation deck. Zack toppled backward and landed on the ground in crab-walk position, completely out of breath.

Zombie Rice rose mechanically off the ground and lumbered relentlessly toward Zack like a demonic windup robot. Rice's jaw hung wide-open, and he let forth a ferocious howl that shook the little punching bag thingy dangling at the back of his throat.

"Dude, what the heck?" Zack backed up on the heels of his palms, huffing and puffing. He scrambled to his feet and sprinted away from Rice to the outdoor storage closet on the deck. Rice approached him, biting the air savagely in front of him as if he were bobbing for apples.

Zack baited himself in front of the door, waiting for Rice to waddle over. "Come on, slowpoke," he said, scrutinizing his friend's zombie walk.

Rice had a pretty good shuffle and a first-rate snarl. Way better than any of his phony zombie impressions. As his rezombified friend neared the closet, Zack leaped swiftly out of the way, shoved Rice inside, and slammed the door shut.

"Phew." Zack sighed and stood for a moment in the semidarkness of the twilit sky. He clapped the dirt off his palms, then bolted inside the skyscraper, hustling to find the others.

At the end of the hallway, Zoe, Madison, and Ozzie were waiting for the elevator.

"You guys." Zack panted, slow to catch his breath. "Come quick. You gotta see this. Rice just—"

"Yo, little bro," Zoe cut him off. "Ms. M and Mrs. G are going to be so ticked off at you guys. You're really late." A big smile stretched across her face. "They'll probably call Mom and Dad on you." Zoe exhaled a self-satisfied sigh. "You're going to be in so much trouble."

"Hate to break it to you," Zack said. "But we're all in trouble."

"Not me," Madison said. "I never get in trouble."

"Yeah, dork brains. We didn't do anything," Zoe said. "You're the one who's gonna get grounded by the parental units."

"Maybe," Zack said. "If Mom and Dad aren't rezombified already."

"Did you just say rezombified?" Ozzie asked.

"Yes, I did, Ozzie," Zack snapped at them all. "It's a

word I just had to make up when my best friend turned back into a flesh-eating mutant and tried to kill me."

"Zack, this really won't be funny if you're joking," said Madison. "We're on vay-cay, okay? Totally not trying to be stressed right now."

"Cross my heart and hope to die!" Zack X'd his chest with one finger and inserted an imaginary needle in his eyeball. "This is serious, you guys!"

"'This is, like, really serious, you guys.'" Zoe mimicked Zack's voice as the three of them reluctantly followed him back to the observation deck.

"That's not even what I said," said Zack, pushing open the door.

Ozzie chuckled. "That was a pretty good Zack impression, though."

"I don't sound like that!" Zack grunted in frustration, grabbing the doorknob. He threw open the closet door to reveal their once unzombified human friend, now their dehumanized zombie friend.

Zombie Rice wobbled in the doorframe with a crooked look on his wild-eyed face and a long blob of slimy mucus dripping from his nose. He cocked his head to the side like a curious kitten. *"Br-ai-ns?"* His voice cracked, gurgling with phlegm.

"Arf!" Twinkles bared his teeth and snarled at the zombie like a well-trained guard dog.

Madison, Ozzie, and Zoe froze in place, all blinking with the same thunderstruck look, totally stupefied by the return of the living dead.

CHAPTER

Zack slammed the door shut and glared at his sister. "Told you so."

"Zachary Arbutus Clarke!" Zoe shouted, snapping out of her shocked stupor. "How could you let this happen?"

"I didn't let anything happen, dodo brain!"

Zoe pointed at the door. "Then what do you call that?"

"I don't know," Zack said. "You in the morning?"

Ozzie chuckled and stuck out his fist, giving Zack a pound of respect. "Good one, bro!"

"Yeah, laugh it up, you little nerdmongers," Zoe said, with fire in her eyes and scorn on her lips. "See what happens."

"Okay, everyone just chill for a second," Zack said, scratching his head. A long silence followed as Zack racked his brain for some possible answers. "It makes sense that Rice would be the first to change back, right?"

"Why's that?" asked Zoe.

"Because," Zack said, "he was the first one to eat the zombie popcorn."

"But that means . . . ," Madison said, petting Twinkles, who sat in her new knockoff designer handbag. "Wait, what does that mean?"

"Probably that the popcorn antidote is wearing off," Ozzie concluded.

"Something like that," said Zack. "Maybe, who knows? But if Rice is rezombified, then it won't be long before everyone who ate the popcorn is going to rezombify, too!"

"All at once . . . ," Ozzie said ominously.

Zack's eyes glazed over as he imagined the possibility of the whole country rezombifying all over again. Ozzie shuddered at the thought, too.

"We don't know that yet, guys," Zoe said, trying to stay positive.

"We don't know anything," said Zack. "Except that Rice is a zombie again."

"I wish Rice was still Rice," Madison said. "He'd totally know why he was a zombie again."

"Well," Zoe said to Madison, "don't just stand there. Go unzombify the little twerp."

Zack reopened the door and took his BZF by the arm. Zoe followed suit and grabbed zombie Rice by his other arm. They wheeled him around like two bouncers escorting a rowdy patron from a nightclub.

"Yarghle-blarghle!" Rice snarled, jerking his head back and forth like a

rabid animal. Ozzie put a bear hug around Rice's knees and lifted him up so his back was parallel with the ground. Zombie Rice squirmed while Madison pricked her finger with a safety pin. She squeezed a drop of blood, the only pure antidote, into his mouth and down his zombie gullet. *Gluggity-glug-glug.*

"There!" she said. "That ought to do it."

And with that they tossed him back in the closet—*bam!* Zack slammed the door shut and they waited for the effect of the dose to transform Rice back into a regular human.

The hinges on the door rattled as Rice thumped away, hyper with rage inside the storage closet.

"He's not unzombifying!" Madison said, with growing alarm in her voice.

"Just give it a minute . . . ," Zack said, trying to stay calm.

Zoe looked at her watch as the seconds ticked by.

But for the next two minutes, Rice kept going more and more berserk. *"Yarghle-blarghle-raaaargh!"*

Ozzie bit his thumbnail and looked nervously at

the three of them. "He should at least be passed out by now."

"Unzombify, you big dummy!" Zoe yelled, slapping the outside of the door loudly.

Zack gazed off into the middle distance, thinking hard for an explanation. And then it hit him like a dodgeball right between the eyes. He gasped and pointed a finger at Madison. "You!"

"Me?" Madison said. "What about me?"

"The pizza we ate earlier," Zack said. "It . . . it must have unveganized your blood or something!"

"That's impossible!" Ozzie said. "She picked the cheese off her pizza. I saw her do it."

"Um." Madison cast her eyes to the ground and mumbled, "I might have had a few nibbles of cheese."

"Madison!" Ozzie cried desperately.

"And maybe, like, a pepperoni—"

"Maybe, like, a *pepperoni*?" Zack asked, throwing his arms up in disbelief.

"I'm sorry," Madison pleaded. "I never tried one before, and Zoe told me it wasn't real meat anyway. By the time I realized she was messing with me, I'd already swallowed it!"

"Zoe!" Ozzie cried, throwing his hands up in the air. "What's the matter with you?"

"How was I supposed to know today was going to be the day that everybody rezombifies?"

Zack gazed forlornly out across the New York skyline. "Guys, do you know what this means?"

"That Madison is supergullible?" Zoe said.

Madison glared at her friend.

"No," Zack said. "It means the party's over."

"Ugh!" Madison pouted and stamped her foot. "I was so getting used to being a national hero."

"Yeah, well, if you want a chance to be a hero again, we're gonna have to stay alive," said Ozzie. "And this time we don't have an antidote, so you'd better listen up."

"Guys, take it easy. We gotta think this through." Zack scratched his chin. "I don't think me and Zoe can rezombify, or Twinkles for that matter." He looked at Madison and Ozzie. "But you two have to be extra careful, because you've both never been zombified before."

"Wait," Ozzie said. "How do we know you guys won't rezombify?"

"Because Zoe and Twinkles got unzombified by Madison directly, and I took the original antidote," Zack said. "Not by the popcorn, like Rice did. Besides, Rice already bit my hand and I'm fine."

"Yeah," said Zoe. "If it's the popcorn antidote wearing off, then it won't affect us."

"Guys," Zack said, shushing the rest of them. "You hear that?"

The group peered down on the city one hundred and two stories beneath them. The *bang-crack* of fender-benders and traffic accidents peppered the air with a noise that resembled a bag of popcorn heating up in the microwave.

"Oh, man," Ozzie said. "There's, like, ten million people in this city, and we're stuck on top of a skyscraper in the middle of Manhattan!"

A chorus of hair-raising shrieks resounded across the boroughs as the groaning wail of the rezombified masses rose up from the city streets below.

A sinking feeling grew fast in the pit of Zack's stomach. *This is bad*, he thought. *Super bad*.

CHAPTER 5

The last rays of daylight vanished beneath the dark red horizon.

Zack, Zoe, Madison, and Ozzie stood atop the skyscraper in the coming darkness before heading back inside.

"Yo," said Zoe. "We needed to get down from here, like, yesterday."

"We can't go down there without a plan," said Zack. "We gotta call Duplessis and see if he knows anything."

"Yeah, I'm not going anywhere until we know what's going on for sure," Madison chimed in. "And neither is Twinkles."

"Ruff-ruff!" Twinkles yapped in agreement, wagging his tail.

Madison pulled out her iPad from her handbag and passed it to Zack.

Zack scrolled through her contacts and found Duplessis. He opened up a video chat on the touch screen and hit send.

There's got to be some way to unzombify Rice, Zack thought as they waited for Duplessis to answer their call.

"I don't understand," Zoe said. "Why isn't he picking up? It's not like he has a whole lot of friends."

"Maybe he's in on it," Ozzie said. "Maybe he planned the whole thing from the start."

"Okay, Mr. Conspiracy Theory," Zoe scoffed. "Now you're starting to sound like Rice."

"Actually," said Madison, making a few zombie noises, "*blargh*! That's what Rice sounds like. . . ."

Just then the door to the women's bathroom flew open with a sharp bang.

"Zack!" Madison shouted. "Watch out!" Zack whipped around as their undead chaperone barreled into the hallway. He leaned away from their rezombi-fied Spanish teacher, but Mrs. Gonzalez was already on him. Her mouth stretched wide, jaws ready to clamp down with her rotting chompers. Her grimy hand shot out and gripped the meat between Zack's neck and shoulder.

"Yow!" Zack cried, as the senora zombie lifted him straight off the ground with a powerful jerk of her arm. Mrs. Gonzalez then clasped her other clammy, bacterial hand around Zack's throat, squeezing off his air supply. Zack's feet dangled inches off the floor as he tried desperately to wedge his fingers between his windpipe and their undead teacher's hands wringing his neck.

Yo tengo problemas," Zack choked.

In the blink of an eye, Ozzie dropped down to a crouch and spun like a breakdancer. He kicked his leg out and the heel of his foot landed cleanly above Mrs. G's ankles, sweeping their rezombified chaperone's legs right out from under her. With a chop of his hand, Ozzie rendered their Spanish teacher unconscious.

Zack stood up and brushed himself off. "Thanks, *amigo*."

"*No problemo*," Ozzie said, and took a bow.

They stashed their conked-out zombie teacher in the bathroom and regrouped out in the hall.

"Hey, you guys, look!" Madison said, picking her iPad off the floor. She held up the screen for everyone to see the video-chat icon flashing. "It's Duplessis!"

"Duplessis!" Zack shouted, taking the iPad from Madison. "Can you hear us?"

Duplessis's chubby little face popped onto the screen. He looked panicked. "Zachary! Zachary! You must get back here. The popcorn antidote is wearing off!"

"We know," said Zack. "What the heck happened?"

"My genetic decoder must have been out-of-date, and the serum it cloned was defective."

"You have got to be kidding me," Zoe scoffed. "Can't we just feed them more of the popcorn or something?"

"I already tried that," Duplessis explained. "But when my zombies ingested it, there was no effect the second time around. They must have built up an immunity!"

"So what are we supposed to do then?" Zack asked.

"Listen to me," Duplessis said. "You have to get Madison back here as soon as possible! If I can get another pure sample, I can fix the problem and concoct a stronger, permanent batch of the zombie popcorn."

"No way, dude," Zoe said. "We went to you last time."

"Seriously," Madison said. "We're not driving all

the way out to Montana again, so you better come to New York and pick us up!"

"Yeah," Ozzie said. "Don't you have a private jet or something?"

"I do, but my pilot's gone and rezombified," Duplessis told them. "I'm under siege!" He panned the webcam over to the door of his sealed-off laboratory. A large crowd of rezombified BurgerDog factory workers pressed their grotesquely mutated faces against the windows of his testing lab, pawing at the glass. "Without a genuine antidote sample, we're all doomed!"

"I hate to be the bearer of bad news," Madison said. "But I ate some pepperoni today and now I kind of sort of can't unzombify zombies anymore."

"Oh, no," Duplessis said. "This is worse than I thought."

"We're really sorry," Zack said. "It was an accident."

"Put Rice on the phone." Duplessis's voice sounded shocked.

"No can do," Ozzie chimed in. "Rice already rezombified."

"How could I have been so stupid?" Duplessis shouted. His head fell to his chest and he began to sob uncontrollably, pulling his wacky skunk hair into a mess of pointed spikes. "Stupid, stupid, stupid!"

"There's really no time to feel sorry for yourself, okay?" Ozzie said. "We need advice."

"Oh, now I get it," Duplessis said between sobs. "You only want to talk to me when you need something, huh?"

"Well, how much of a sample are we talking here?" Zack asked, trying to stay focused.

"A drop, a speck, a molecule!" the fast-food geneticist yelled in despair. Just then Duplessis turned away from the webcam. Zack and the gang watched the scene unfold on the iPad as the rezombified BurgerDog factory workers busted into his laboratory, ripping the doors right off the hinges.

Duplessis turned back to the video chat, his eyes wide with fright, as the zombies started to funnel through the doorway.

"What do we do?" Zack yelled.

"Find more vegans and give them that gingko water!" Duplessis shouted. "We should be able to simulate another antidote serum just as effective as Madison's. . . ."

The rezombified BurgerDog employees thrashed across the room, sweeping beakers and test tubes off the tabletops and sending them crashing to the floor.

"Gotta go," Duplessis said quickly. "Before these zombies give me an encephalotomy!" He turned his attention to one of his experiments about to get trashed by a rampaging zombie. "Hey, you, get away from there! Don't touch that. That's my brand-new formula for a sour-cream-and-onion-flavored sports drink!" The BurgerDog creator raced out of the frame, knocking the webcam to the floor.

A second later, the connection cut off, and the touch screen turned bright blue.

BurgerDog was officially back in business.

The zombie-making business.

CHAPTER 6

ack stared down blankly at the iPad. "What the heck are we gonna do now?" he said, handing the tablet back to Madison. "We're right back at square one."

Ozzie scratched his head. "I wonder where the airport is around here?"

"What's it matter?" Zack said. "You think we're just going to round up some vegans and jet off to Montana? Where are we supposed to find real human specimens right now? Ninety-nine-point-nine percent of the population got unzombified by the popcorn. We're the lucky ones."

"Yeah, real lucky." Madison rolled her eyes.

"My point is that we can't just go running into the return of the living dead without a plan. We're in New York City and we've got zilch! No weapons, no antidote." Zack turned to Zoe. "Because earlier today somebody had to trick Madison into eating a pepperoni!"

"Don't you dare, you little worm," Zoe snapped. "I will not be your scapegoat!"

"Oh, you're some kind of goat, all right!" Zack shouted.

"Come on." Ozzie grabbed Zoe's hand and put it back down. "We have to stick together if we're going to get out of this mess."

"Well, I'm not going anywhere until I get a new Band-Aid," Madison said, pinching her pricked finger. "There's no way I'm getting infected with slime and turning into one of those zombie freaks."

A long silence followed, punctuated by zombie Rice's banging on the inside of the closet door. The gears in Zack's head turned, his thoughts whirling frantically to come up with a solution. *Bingo.*

"That's it!" he shouted with a sudden flash of hope. "The Band-Aid!"

"Yes," Madison said. "I need one."

"No," said Zack. "I'm talking about the Band-Aid you had on before you ate the pizza!"

Madison gasped, realizing what he meant. "It has my vegan blood on it! Zack, you're a genius!"

"We gotta go back to Central Park, you guys," Zack said. "Come on, help me zombie-proof Rice!"

Zack and Zoe dragged zombie Rice out of the closet and hog-tied him with Twinkles's pink Bedazzled collar and leash. Ozzie found some duct tape in the storage closet and used it to tape the King Kong mask securely over Rice's head.

Rice wriggled his zombified tongue through the little hole in the mouth of the gorilla mask, searching around like a nose sniffing at the air. "Not quite as good as a helmet," Ozzie said. "But it'll have to do."

Lastly, Ozzie duct-taped Rice's hands behind his back. The girls pulled him by the leash into the elevator and Zack and Ozzie followed. As the elevator descended, Rice snapped his teeth and snarled his lips in time with the Muzak playing on the overhead speakers.

A few seconds into the ride, Zack pinched his nostrils shut. "Yo, who did that?"

"Don't look at me!" Ozzie said. "I didn't do it!"

"Ha," Zoe said. "Whoever denied it supplied it."

"Whoever smelt it dealt it." Ozzie pointed at Zack.

"You're both wrong," said Zack. "Whoever said the rhyme committed the crime."

"Will you guys shut up?" Madison said. "It's Rice. He's already starting to stink!"

"Yuck!" They all plugged their noses, glaring at zombie Rice as the elevator reached the first floor of the Empire State Building.

Three . . . two . . . one.

The doors of the elevator opened and they stared out across the ground floor.

The lobby teemed with rezombified freaks. The

claustrophobic mass was a mix of their classmates, building employees, tourists, and New Yorkers. Dozens of subhuman beings dribbled ooze and drooled slime as they lumbered aimlessly across the smooth marble floor.

Zack hit the door-close button and held the elevator. "Whoa!" He turned to the others. "There are a lot of zombies out there!"

"Okay, guys and girls, it's go time," Ozzie said, unclipping his nunchakus from his belt buckle. He gripped both handles and flexed the chain. "We gotta get Rice across the lobby, through those revolving doors, and out into the street. Ready?"

"Set . . . ," said Zack, pressing the elevator button.

Ding!

The doors flung open and the zombies turned and glared as the gang charged out of the elevator.

"Here we go!" Ozzie lunged forward and unleashed a furious nunchaku attack at the zombified doorman standing in his way. The doorman's graying face mashed over to the side as if it were made of wet clay, and the great goon dropped like a rag doll.

Ozzie caught the unconscious zombie midfall and heaved him into the oncoming zombie foot slog.

Nom-nom! Glurp!

Next to him, Zoe kickboxed her way through a slew of flesh-guzzling tourists, taking out two teenage zombie siblings wearing I ❤ NY T-shirts with a flurry of punch-kick combos. As Zoe and Ozzie cleared a path through the kill-crazy melee, Zack yanked the leash, guiding Rice forward, while Madison kept him on a bee-line for the exit.

Just then a hot-pink backpack came out of nowhere and slammed Zack directly in the chest. "Ugh!" Zack lost his grip on Rice's leash as he stumbled back with the wind knocked out of him. He slipped on a wet splotch of mucus and landed on his tailbone with a hard thud. Zack winced in pain, clutching his back.

The pink-backpacked zombie spun around, snarling fiercely. It was Mandy Pitman, his classmate and one of the Fearsome Foursome. Her claws were shiny bright crimson daggers from her red nail polish. She pounced at Zack, who went flat on his back and lifted his knees. He caught the zombie mean girl with the soles of his feet and leg-pressed her against the wall with a double kick. The undead brat hit the wall and slid to the floor in a motionless lump of twisted, rotting flesh.

"Sorry!" Zack shouted.

"Rargh!"

Zack turned his head and flinched as a second member of the foursome staggered through the undead mayhem. The queen bee herself, Gabby Kahn, lurched over Zack. "Glargh!" He brought his leg back again and delivered a sharp kick to her kneecap, which bent back the wrong way. She dropped to the floor and crawled forward, dragging her dead leg behind her, leaving a trail of slime in her wake.

"Madison!" Zack yelled as zombie Rice came back into view. "Watch out!"

"Rargh!" Zombie Rice reeled around and barreled into Madison, who stumbled and fell with a splat in a pool of slimy zombie ooze.

"Ugh!" Madison screeched, watching zombie Rice

wander into the undead mix. "These shoes are brand-new!" As she scrambled to her feet, a fiendish trio of seventh-grade math geeks began to converge around her.

She tucked Twinkles in the crook of her arm, then flung her handbag at the three zombie dweebs and

raced across the lobby through the horde of mutant hellhounds.

"Zack, Madison, come on!" Ozzie yelled, knocking a zombie businessman on his rear end with a hard punch to the gut. "Hurry up!" Ozzie and Zoe bobbed

and weaved like dueling prizefighters, fending off three more corporate zombies in suits and ties. The undead businessmen flailed their arms wildly, wielding their briefcases clasped firmly in their arthritic fists.

"We're not leaving Rice!" yelled Zack as he scrambled to his feet.

"We'll come back for him!" Zoe yelled from across the lobby.

"No way!" Zack shouted, and dashed back into the swarm of knuckle-dragging cranium eaters. Zack ran low to the ground, trying to stay under the zombies' brain-sensing infrared. He set his sights on Rice's leash dragging on the floor and darted forward, snatching it up. Zack yanked the leash as hard as he could and caught zombie Rice off guard. Rice's gorilla head snapped back and his feet kicked into the air as he slammed to the floor with a *thunk*. Zack pulled the leash, lugging zombie Rice behind him across the slime-slick marble floor.

As Zack neared the revolving door, their zombified chaperone Ms. Merriweather staggered in front of him.

"Bleckch-argh!" she gurgled, and grabbed for him. Zack stepped right and spun left. The zombie music teacher went for the fake, bear-hugging the air and missing Zack completely.

Zack held the leash tight as Rice glided along the floor, swinging right at the back of Ms. Merriweather's knees like a tripwire.

Their zombified chaperone flipped into the air, head over heels, and hit the floor, landing with a loud crunch in a twisted heap of dislocated joints.

Zack quickly crammed himself in the glass compartment with zombie Rice and pushed them through the revolving door.

The rest of the zombie crowd plowed up the lobby behind Ms. Merriweather, snarling and retching, gargling their own saliva.

Zoe and Madison were waiting outside on the sidewalk as Zack pulled Rice through the rotating exit. Just then Ozzie came out of nowhere, wheeling a bicycle.

"Heads up!" he yelled, and jammed the bike into the revolving door before the zombies inside the building could turn it into an undead scary-go-round.

"Thanks, Oz!" Zack said, patting him on the shoulder.

"No prob," Ozzie said. "That bike should hold them off."

"Okay," Zoe said. "But what about them?"

They all turned toward the street and gazed into the frantic bedlam of rezombified Manhattan. The rancid funk of accelerated decay brewed thickly in the air, making Zack gag.

"Come on," Zoe said, pointing down the sidewalk. "This way!"

They took off racing into the plague-ridden metropolis as if there was no tomorrow.

CHAPTER

An infinite herd of rezombified brain gobblers shifted through the New York City streets. Vapors of hot stench squiggled off the massive heaps of uncollected restaurant garbage piled along the curb. Fresh produce spilled from the cardboard boxes littered around the fallen fruit stands. Dangerous arrays of lemons and limes rolled out across the sidewalk as the rot-ripened hordes trampled through every nook and cranny of the city looking for human flesh and brains.

Ozzie and Zoe flanked Madison and Zack as they maneuvered Rice down the sidewalk.

"Hey, guys, look over there!" shouted Madison, who was pointing at an empty beat-up shopping cart sitting in front of a street vendor's demolished table. The sidewalk was scattered with hats, purses, umbrellas, and shiny iPhone cases.

As they approached the table, Zack ran over and rolled the cart back to where Rice stood wobbling on his leash.

"Ozzie," Zack called over the crescendo of undead moans. "Help me lift him up!"

Zack and Ozzie lifted Rice up by his underarms, which now were sopping wet from zombie Rice's over-heated sweat glands.

"Ew!" Ozzie said with a sour look on his face.

The boys dropped their friend in disgust and Rice landed bottom-first in the cart. With his hands duct-taped behind his back, there was no way zombie Rice was getting out.

"Okay, guys, let's gear up!" said Zack, taking an armful of umbrellas from the bin next to the table. He held on to one and stuffed the other two in the shopping cart with Rice. Zoe and Madison picked a stack of hardcover books out of a grimy brown milk crate and loaded the books into two faux-leather handbags from the pile of merchandise. Ozzie twirled his nunchakus, getting ready for the battle, and the girls gave their weighted handbags a couple of practice swings.

The cheap leather swooshed heavily through the air.

Holding his umbrella, Zack spotted a twenty-something zombie girl wearing hot-pink jeans and a black tank top stumbling toward them, licking her chops in a mindless daze of brain lust. Zack thrust out the curved handle of the umbrella and hooked the ghoulish cannibal around the ankle. He yanked back hard, pulling the zombie's feet right out from under her. "I think this is gonna work," Zack said, looking at the others, now armed for the zombie street brawl.

They were ready to roll, and so without a second to lose, they pushed forward into the zombie groundswell.

Zack crouched low and gripped his umbrella, sneaking stealthily through the vehicular maze of crashed and abandoned cars, careful not to look the mad cannibal zombies directly in the eye.

They moved down the street undetected for the moment, but before they knew it, an undead, heavyset Gypsy woman caught sight of them as she stumbled out of her tiny shop marked PALM & TAROT READING. The zombie fortune-teller gazed into Zack's brainless future, hobbling toward him with her arms outstretched. Her ankles were bird-thin, and her calves were thick as ham hocks. As she lumbered toward them, her ankle snapped under her own weight and she fell, smashing her kneecap on the pavement like a dropped crystal ball. Zack juked around the crippled Gypsy and sped up along with the rest of the group.

Up ahead, Fifth Avenue was completely gridlocked with crashed automobiles. The sidewalks teemed with countless hundreds of plug-ugly brain munchers roaming ravenously through the streets.

"Down here, guys!" Ozzie shouted, signaling them away from the bottleneck on Fifth Avenue.

They headed west on Thirty-fourth Street, where the zombie foot traffic was slightly less dense. Zack trailed Zoe, who was pushing Rice in the shopping cart. Madison held Twinkles under one arm and swung her weighted handbag at a rezombified construction worker stumbling off the curb. The heavy bag landed squarely on the side of the zombie's blister-pocked face and the brute toppled over.

"Nice shot!" Zack shouted, sprinting past her.

As they came to the end of the block, Zoe halted the shopping cart and stopped in the middle of the street. Zack ran into the intersection and spun around three hundred and sixty degrees, taking in the nightmarish scene.

A vast array of rezombified mongrels jammed up Sixth Avenue, and let out a collective feral yowl from the depths of their esophagi, spraying oodles of rank mucus into the air like science-fair volcanoes.

"Zoe, look out!" Madison yelled.

"Duck!" cried Zack as a large cobweb of spittle sailed through the air.

Ozzie dived and tackled Zoe out of the way as the venomous gobbet of zombie saliva flew by their heads and splattered on the ground with an acidic hiss.

"Over here!" They all followed Ozzie's lead, running toward the northwest corner, where a huge building bore an enormous red sign with a big white star and white font claiming THE LARGEST STORE IN THE WORLD.

The undead New Yorkers were closing in from

all directions. They had to get off the streets immediately.

Zack pushed Rice in the cart behind Ozzie, Madison, and his sister as they ran onto the sidewalk. He charged up the grooved cement ramp, accidentally crashing the front of the cart into a tipped-over garbage can.

"Yarghkle!" Rice gurgled behind his gorilla mask, wedged uncomfortably in the rattling cart.

Zack stopped on the corner and peered up at either side of the gigantic block. North, south, east, west, all ways looked identical, packed to the gills with a gazillion savage hellhounds.

Macy's was their only refuge.

Ozzie raced over and held open the double doors, waving them inside the store. Zack carted zombie Rice into the vestibule, and Madison and Zoe scurried in after him. Ozzie jumped inside last, and Zack pinned the shopping cart flush against the glass doors, keeping the zombies at bay outside.

The girls stood for a brief moment on the threshold

of the vast department store. "Hold down the fort, Zack!" Zoe said, casing the joint. "We'll be back before you can say, 'Where the heck did my way cooler older sister go?'"

"We don't have any time for shopping!" Zack yelled angrily over the undead panting and groans echoing loudly through the doors.

"Don't be ridiculous," said Madison. "There's always time for a little shopping."

"Zoe, come on," said Zack. "Please, let's just stick together."

"Zack," she said. "We can take care of ourselves."

"Yeah," said Madison. "And besides, these heels are simply not cutting it." She lifted up one of her feet and Zack crinkled his nose at the black zombie slime caked on the mangled heel of her shoe.

"Fine," Zack said. "But you're leaving Twinkles with us. Remember last time?"

"Whatevs," they said in unison. Madison handed Twinkles to Zack. "Come on, Mad. Let's go get some new kicks." The girls joined hands and skipped off happily toward the shoe section of the department store.

"Don't worry about them," Ozzie said. "Can you get me something to secure the door? Check if Rice has anything in his pack."

Zack flipped zombie Rice over in the shopping cart while Ozzie leaned his weight into the handlebar, trying to keep out the herd of zombie chowhounds piled against the glass entrance.

Zack reached into Rice's pack and the first thing he pulled out was a plain bologna sandwich. *Yuck!* He tossed it away and reached back in.

The zombies began to squeeze their mangled hands in the gap between the glass doors.

"Hurry!" Ozzie said, pressing the shopping cart harder against the entrance.

Zack rooted his hand around all the way to the bottom of the bag and extracted a Kryptonite bicycle lock with a small key dangling from it.

"Perfect!" Zack said, latching the handles on the double doors together with the metal lock. Ozzie pulled the shopping cart away from the door, safe with the bike lock holding the zombie swarm at bay.

Twinkles trotted ahead of the boys into Macy's, prancing across the linoleum floor, his little puppy snout wiggling around, sniffing the air. Suddenly Twinkles stopped midstride and lifted one paw up like a hunting dog pointing to a kill. The Boggle pup barked once, aiming his paw at a clothing rack across the store.

Ozzie approached the row of garment racks cautiously and— "Blargh!" A zombie saleslady popped out, ripping down clothes hangers and thrashing designer blouses to the floor.

The undead saleswoman charged at Ozzie, but

he danced back and sidestepped the zombie's attack. He grabbed her arm and twisted it with expert precision, then pivoted his body into her rib cage and flipped her over his back and onto the floor with a terrific thud.

"Ozzie!" Zack called. "Stay close, man! You can't afford to get bitten, remember?"

"Chill out, Zack," Ozzie called back. "Me and Twinkles got this!"

Ozzie and Twinkles continued to hunt stray zombie shoppers and store workers throughout the racks of clothes and around the counters, securing the area.

Just then, Zack caught a whiff of Rice's rank zombie stench and pinched his nose. "Man, you stink," he said, and carted his monkey-headed zombie friend over to the perfume counters.

"How about this one?" Zack asked. He opened one of the cologne bottles and sniffed the spray nozzle. Then he spritzed a puff of cologne on Rice's tongue. Zombie Rice spit it back in Zack's face, making a "yuck" sound.

"Ugh, man!" Zack said, whipping the zombie spittle off his face.

Zack took a whiff of another fragrance. "Actually, let's go with this one." He clicked the spritzer repeatedly, dousing Rice with more cheap cologne than a seventh-grade date dance.

Zack inhaled deeply through his nose and choked a little. *Much better*, he thought. Then he glanced around, keenly aware that Ozzie and Twinkles were out of sight. Madison and Zoe were taking way too long, too.

All of a sudden, a blast of shattered glass sounded behind him. The door they had barricaded with Rice's bike lock was being destroyed by the mass of zombies kicking and bashing into the department store like a mad rush of Black Friday bargain hunters.

"Guys!" Zack shouted. "We gotta roll! Guys?"

The jabbering nitwits thrashed around the store, barking and snorting, grunting and flailing in an all-consuming state of madness.

Suddenly Zack heard an ear-piercing screech coming from deep in the store. "Zoe! Madison!" He jogged toward the sound of the girly shriek, pushing the cart in a thick smog of zombie BO and men's perfume.

Just then Zoe sprinted around the corner with Madison. "Yo, little bro!" yelled Zoe. "We gotta peace out! They got some messed-up-lookin' ladies in the lingerie department!"

"Yeah, for real! Good thing we went shoe shopping first," Madison said. "Check these out." She curtsied, showing off her new kicks. "They're from this really cool company call Bio-Wear, made from one hundred percent vegan-friendly materials. They're local, too. Made in Brooklyn by real live Brooklynites. Isn't that cool?"

"Sorry, Madison," Zack said. "I don't care about that right now. Where's Ozzie?"

"I'm here!" Ozzie shouted, charging in with Twinkles. "We gotta bounce!" he said, pointing at the zombie swarm pouring in through the broken door.

"Yeah," Zack said. "No kidding, Sherlock!"

"Come on. This way!" Zoe yelled, and took the lead running. "There's another exit over here."

Zack grabbed the handlebar of the shopping cart–turned–zombie stroller, and hurried to the other side of the store. They pushed through the exit, back out into the chaos on the sidewalks of New York.

CHAPTER

The New York City buildings towered above them like the walls of an inescapable labyrinth. Zack stood on the sidewalk and looked both ways down the darkened street. The zombies raged through the city top to bottom. High up in offices and apartment buildings, the windows were a shadow-puppet horror show of brain-sick mayhem and mindless destruction. Gaggles of rancorous undead brain gluttons howled like rabid chimpanzees in locked laboratory cages.

"Which way are we supposed to go?" asked Madison.

"We gotta get back to Central Park," Zack yelled. "Which way is north?"

"Hold on," said Ozzie as he calculated due north.

Zoe opened up one of the umbrellas and held it over Ozzie's head. "You're welcome," she said.

"For what?" Ozzie asked. Then a bucketload of zombie slime rained down from seven stories up, where an undead apartment dweller upchucked off his balcony. The putrid bile splattered on the umbrella, sparing Ozzie a slime shower.

"Thanks," Ozzie said, and then pointed to one end of the street. "Down there! We've gotta make a right at the next intersection."

They raced down the street and hung a right. Ozzie and Zoe sprinted off the curb and into the street. Madison ran slightly ahead of Zack, and Twinkles trailed through the puddles of sludge as they raced north up Seventh Avenue, dipping and dodging through the jam-packed mishmash of flesh-hungry mutants.

Zack hopped onto the hood of a parked car, ran up the windshield, and paused, standing on the roof. From there, he had a much better viewpoint, but it did them no good. They were caught in a bobble-headed sea of slime-dribbling zombie noggins. Looking farther ahead, Zack could see a colorful array of neon lights dazzling at the end of the block. *Times Square*, Zack thought with a shudder. He ran down the back of the automobile and bounded off the bumper. His feet hit the pavement and he dashed away from the riptide of slime-splattering ghouls pushing up the rear.

When they reached the next intersection, the cityscape changed.

The buildings in Times Square scraped the sky, flashing with huge video billboards that dazzled the zombie nightlife with a flickering digital glow. It was the personification of carnage. Zombies' faces bubbled and ruptured with boils. Their hands dangled at their sides, chins jutting forward as they bit at the air with such ferocity that their grinding teeth began to crack and crumble until all that was left were jagged shards of enamel rooted in their decaying gums.

A perfect storm of zombie mobs filled the streets, converging on the intersection where Zack and the gang now froze undead in their tracks. All around him, Zack saw nothing but a blur of slack-jawed faces, walking blobs of rotting goo swaying side to side on rubbery legs.

Over to Zack's left, two wicked zombies from a nearby Broadway musical tottered out from an alley-way still in full stage makeup. The undead performers circled Ozzie in their winged monkey costumes. Ozzie lunged forward and whapped a monkey man with his nunchaku, then danced back easily before clashing with the other rezombified actor. *Whap-whap!*

"Ozzie, look out!" Zoe called as a third wicked flying monkey staggered out from behind a hot-dog stand. She took a running start and blasted the other zombie with a blow from her handbag that sent him reeling off balance headfirst into a mailbox on the curbside. Ozzie and Zoe high-fived and swiveled back to Zack and Madison, who stood shell-shocked in the eye of the zombie maelstrom.

The diverse zombie crowd was dressed in every imaginable fashion: T-shirts and jeans, shorts and tank tops, suits, ties, sundresses, polo shirts, khakis, postal uniforms, construction helmets, bike helmets, and spandex, all dragging their sneakers, sandals, and loafers through the streets.

Ozzie took a step and leaped straight up, grabbing the bars underneath a DON'T WALK sign. Hanging by his arms from a street pole, Ozzie swung back and pumped forward with both legs. *Pow!* He landed a powerful two-footed kick into the chest of a thickset, middle-aged zombie tourist sporting an entire outfit made out of blue denim. The denim-clad zombie flew back into the impenetrable horde.

DON'T
WALK

As the undead mob continued its slow-footed rampage, Zack felt the bass-heavy thump of pop music coming from a nearby nightclub.

The walking corpses began to twitch in unison, closing in on Zack, Madison, Zoe, Ozzie, and Twinkles. The zombies' feet began to shuffle in step to the beat, and their undead shoulders started to swivel.

The King of Pop's voice taunted them: "And no one's gonna save you from the beasts about to strike!"

As the thickly packed zombie flash dancers corralled them tighter into the neon nightmare of Times Square after dusk, Zack felt a kick of panic in his gut. He looked all around, but there was no escape from the undead flash mob homing in on them from all directions.

Ozzie charged into the crowd as two college-age girls

in miniskirts and bright yellow-and-lime-green halter tops latched onto his arms. Ozzie raised his nunchaku to take them out, but as he did, their boyfriends stepped to the forefront of the crowd. The two zombie juiceheads wore tight black muscle shirts that hugged their torsos. The *Jersey Shore* wannabes shimmied forward, protecting their zombified dates, moonwalking simultaneously between

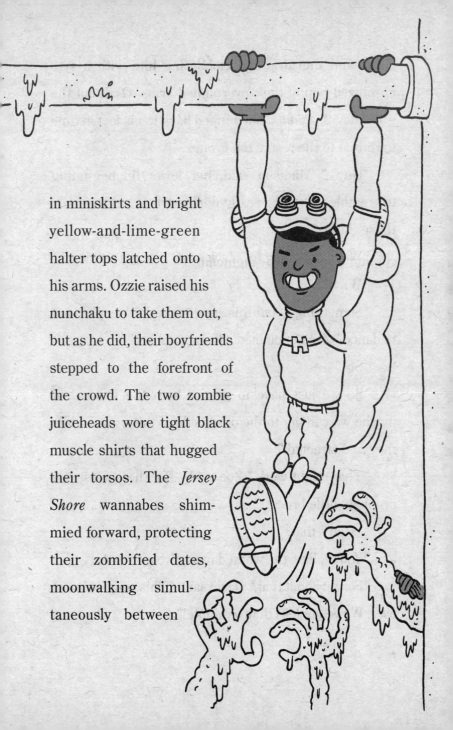

Ozzie and the girls and clobbering him with a synchronized pop of their overtanned arms. Ozzie hit the ground with a *thunk*, but jumped back to his feet in time to retreat to the rest of the group.

"Guys," Madison said, her lower lip beginning to tremble. "I really, really don't want to get eaten by these things!"

"We're not going to," Zack said. "I've got an idea."

"What?"

"Something about this song makes all people want to dance," Zack explained. "Even zombies."

"So?"

"So we just have to groove with the music and maybe we can get to the other side of this crowd while they're distracted."

"That might work," Zoe said. "But there's just one problem, little bro. . . ."

"What's that?"

"You're, like, the worst dancer I've ever seen!"

"Forget about that," Ozzie said. "This song's almost over. We've got less than a minute!"

With that, Zack grabbed the handle of the shopping cart. Zombie Rice wiggled his hips to the beat of the music and bounced his shoulders. As they all busted out their best zombified dance moves, they tried to pinpoint the least congested spot in the most lopsided game of Red Rover any of them had ever played.

Zack carted zombie Rice through the zombie flash mob, keeping his steps in time with the song's rhythm. On either side of the shopping cart, Madison raised the roof, while Zoe twisted and shouted as the zombified boogie monsters hand-jived around them.

"It's working," Ozzie said, shaking his booty at an undead moonwalker gliding his feet across the sludge-coated blacktop.

Suddenly the familiar pop song ended and a different song drifted out from the nightclub. The zombies stopped dancing for a moment and snapped out of their trance. Now the four of them were stuck in the middle of a massive herd of flesh-craving gluttons. But they had made it far enough.

"Look!" Zoe cried, pointing across the street. "The subway!"

And with no other choice but down, they raced over to the steps of the subway station and descended underground, lugging Rice's shopping cart into the bowels of the city.

CHAPTER 3

The walls of the subway were grime-black and smeared with mucus-y green and yellow driblets oozing through the cracks in the concrete ceiling. The smell down there was suffocating, and Zack covered his mouth and nose, inhaling through the fabric of his shirt. Madison and Zoe did the same, gasping and coughing through the thick, hot underground stench.

As they reached the turnstiles of the subway station, Zack peered over his shoulder and caught a glimpse of the massive throng of undead brainmongers waddling down the subway steps behind them.

Ozzie bounded over the turnstiles and hurled open the emergency door. The alarm shrieked and Zack pushed Rice through. Madison and Zoe ducked under the turnstiles and the four of them halted on the platform.

Twinkles lapped his tongue happily at a puddle of zombie slime.

"Ew, Twinkles, gross!" Madison cried, picking up her pup.

On the other side of the tracks, a mass of zombies tottered on the opposite platform, groping through the air frantically, moaning in agony for a bit of live human flesh.

Standing on the edge of the subway platform, Zack swiveled his head in all directions. "Quick," Zack said. "We need a plan."

"Down there!" Madison shouted, pointing toward another exit at the opposite end of the subway platform.

They raced toward the exit, but as soon as they reached the bottom step, a dense bunch of undead cannibals came crushing down the staircase, heading right for them.

The kids retreated and stopped dead in their tracks, trapped between two converging zombie mobs.

"We could take the tunnel . . . ," Ozzie suggested. "The trains probably aren't running."

They peered over the edge, looking down on a stream of dirty garbage water flowing down the train tracks. Near the threshold of the tunnel, a roiling herd of undead rats and cockroaches churned relentlessly in the pit of subway filth.

"Are you kidding?" Madison squealed. "I'd rather get my brains eaten!"

"What other choice do we have?" said Ozzie.

The first zombie mob struggled to fit through the turnstiles behind them, no thanks to a bloated zombie at the head of the pack stuck firmly in the center lane.

His midsection was so gigantic that it looked like he had swallowed a wrecking ball, and he wore a blue triple-XL T-shirt that gave him the appearance of a walking piece of M&M's candy. The sumo-size zombie's lips retracted back in a broad psychotic smile, showing off a crooked row of chompers blackened at the root.

Zoe ran forward, pushing the shopping cart into the zombified turnstiles. The big blue M&M's monster man thrashed in a burst of zombie superstrength. *Pow!* The metal turnstile snapped off, unleashing a surge of undead subway dwellers onto the platform. Zoe jumped back and the shopping cart tipped onto its side. Zombie Rice spilled out, rolling past the yellow caution line and over the ledge to the tracks below.

"Rice!" Zack yelled, rushing to keep his friend from falling, but Rice had already landed in a rank puddle of muck.

Zack and Ozzie jumped down fast and pulled Rice up to his feet, while the girls fended off the oncoming zombies.

"Madison, Zoe!" yelled Zack, standing on the tracks below. "Come on. We don't have a choice!"

Just then, Twinkles made a little whinnying sound as the tunnel began to vibrate with a distant rumble.

"There's a train coming!" Madison screamed. "Get off the tracks!"

"Grab his arms!" Zack shouted, lifting Rice up with Ozzie. The girls crouched down on the platform and reached over, gripping Rice by his wrists, while Zack and Ozzie pushed Rice back up to safety.

Ozzie planted the palms of his hands on the platform edge and hoisted himself back onto the platform.

He stood up and reached a helping hand down to Zack just as a pair of headlights appeared from the depths of the subway tunnel.

Zack moved forward to reach for Ozzie's hand, but his foot was wedged between the rusted metal rails of the track.

"Zack!" yelled Zoe. "Come on!"

"I can't," he cried desperately. "I'm stuck."

The subway train screeched its brakes, honking its horn.

"Somebody do something!" Madison shrieked.

Zack pulled his leg up again, but the sneaker wouldn't budge. He froze like a deer in headlights.

Ozzie jumped back down onto the tracks and crouched by Zack's feet to loosen his shoelaces. Zack wriggled free of the shoe completely and they hopped back onto the zombifying platform as the train sped toward them. Zack wiped the sweat from his brow and sucked in a long, beautiful breath of rank-smelling air, thankful to be alive.

The train halted and the conductor slid his window open and stuck his head out. "What the heck are you waiting for?" he said. "Get on!"

The doors popped open and Ozzie and Zoe shoved zombie Rice inside. Madison hopped on the train car with Twinkles, holding the door for Zack. "Come on, Zack!" Ozzie yelled.

"One sec!" Zack shouted, and sprinted back to their tipped-over shopping cart. He sneaked between two

zombies clawing for his head and snatched up as much of their bootleg weaponry as he could.

"Coming through!" Zack yelled, elbowing his way through the zombies and diving between the closing doors. Madison and Zoe jumped out of the way as Zack landed on the floor of the train. He breathed a sigh of relief as the cadaverous brain hounds smacked the outside of the moving subway car.

CHAPTER 10

As the train accelerated into the underground tunnel, the headlights cast a pale yellow glow through the darkness. Zoe hitched Rice's leash to a pole and pointed at him. "Stay right there, you bad little monkey."

Zack, now missing a shoe, took one off Rice's foot and put on the mismatched sneaker. They walked through the connecting door into the front of the train, where the conductor sat at the controls.

"Up to Eighty-first, sir," said Zoe. "And step on it!"

"Now just wait a minute, little lady," he said, turning around. "This train ain't making no more stops.

You're lucky I picked you up at all. Thought you were a couple of zombies until I recognized you little rascals from the TV."

"You know who we are?" Zack asked.

"Course I do," he said. "You're those kids I keep seeing on the news who killed all them zombies!"

"Not killed," Madison said. "Saved."

"Whatever," said the conductor. "You're all kinds of famous."

"Hear that?" Zoe said, nudging Madison excitedly. "We're still famous. . . ."

"You got a name, sir?" Ozzie asked the man.

"Cecil," he said, pronouncing the name "see-sill."

"Well, thanks for saving us back there, Cecil," Zack said.

He looked at them sincerely. "Old Cecil'd do anything to help out a couple of national heroes, any day of the dog-garn week."

"Then you have to drop us off at Eighty-first Street, sir," said Zack. "It's our only hope of getting the antidote to stop all this mess!"

"Oh, all right," he said. "I think you're crazy, but I guess you have your reasons."

"Great," Zack said. "How much farther?"

"Just about three more stops after this one," Cecil said, pointing out the window as they whizzed past another zombified subway platform.

"Thanks, Cecil!" Madison and Zoe said together.

"Oh, don't thank me. If it wasn't for you little rascals, Old Cecil'd still be a zombie."

"You were a zombie?" Zack asked.

"Yeah," he said. "Until I ate that popcorn I was."

Before Zack could process the dark realization creeping into his brain, the conductor retched and flopped forward, hitting the controls.

The train accelerated at a breakneck pace. Zack punched the buttons, and Ozzie yanked back on the handle, but the lever snapped off from the control panel and the subway topped max speed.

"Blaaarghhh!"

Cecil reanimated from his slumped position, craning his neck and jutting his jaw. The muckle-mouthed fiend hissed demonically and stared blankly at them with its white pupil-less eyes.

"Ahhhh!" Zoe, Zack, Ozzie, and Madison all screamed and retreated out of the subway cockpit, piling back into the train car where Rice was tied to the pole.

The zombie conductor clambered out of the subway cockpit, raking his claws through the air, swiping for their heads.

Zack unknotted the leash and pulled Rice toward him while Ozzie and the girls all grabbed their weapons. As the train zipped past the next subway stop, the zombie conductor rushed toward them in a frenzied outburst of deep-throated growls and belly-bumped Zack with the sack of blubber hanging over his waistband. Zack held Rice up like a zombie shield before backing farther to the middle of the subway car.

"Whoa, Nelly!" Zoe shouted, looking down at the other end of the train. The doors split open and a horde of zombie passengers crushed up the aisle and staggered toward them leeringly.

Zoe opened up one of the umbrellas and charged

forward, slamming it into the zombies, pushing them back.

In the middle of the train, Ozzie and Madison wedged their fingernails in between the doors of the subway car, trying to pull them apart manually.

The too-fast train rocked back and forth violently, and Zack had to plant his heels to steady himself, riding the floor of the subway car as if it were a surfboard.

The light in the subway brightened as they zipped past another platform. "Two more to go!" Ozzie shouted.

A zombie old-timer with a long beard lumbered

down the moving train car. He wore Bermuda shorts with suspenders over a T-shirt, and New Balance sneakers with high dress socks pulled up to his knees. The undead senior citizen snatched Madison by her forearm with both hands and clamped his slobbering maw down onto her flesh.

"Ahhhhh!" Madison screamed, anticipating the sharp pain of pierced skin and the prospect of her perfect face undergoing zombification. But all she felt was the dull clamp from the zombie's toothless gums.

She pried her arm out of the chomperless zombie's mouth and knocked him in his noggin with her elbow.

That was a close one! Zack thought as he tightened up the slack on Rice's leash.

The subway shot through the tunnel like a bullet. The train car jostled and jerked, bumping the zombies off balance as it hurtled by the last subway stop before Eighty-first street.

Madison lifted her leg and kicked another zombie coming down the center of the aisle, while Ozzie pried at the door.

"It's not opening," Ozzie yelled.

The Central Park subway stop was fast approaching. The zombies inched closer and closer. Twinkles barked and yipped ferociously, circling their rotting feet.

Zack took the metal tip of the umbrella and jammed it between the doors like a crowbar. He jerked the umbrella to one side and the doors flung open on the moving train.

"Everybody jump!" Zack grabbed zombie Rice by the leash and the five of them leaped off the train at the last second. They hit the subway platform and rolled as the zombified train flew roaring past.

"Everyone okay?" Zack asked, brushing himself off.

"Where's Twinkles?" Madison cried, and they all looked out at the train hurtling forward. Twinkles was still perched in the open doors of the subway car, too timid to jump.

Madison scrambled to her feet, racing after the runaway train. "Twinkles!" she called. "Come!"

Twinkles barked and wiggled his rump, then took a flying leap as the train shot into the tunnel. The little pup landed on the platform unscathed and pranced toward Madison. She clutched Twinkles to her chest and pressed her cheek to the little Boggle, who was now happily licking her ear.

"You okay, Mad?" Zoe asked her BFF.

"Mm-hmm," Madison lied, biting her bottom lip to stop it from quivering.

Twinkles made a little whimpering noise and barked twice at his master.

"Uh-oh," Zoe said, examining her friend.

"What?" Zack and Ozzie asked simultaneously.

"You might want to back up," Zoe said. "She's gonna have a meltdown."

"Well, what do you expect?" Madison broke into tears, sobbing. "We almost just lost Twinkles. And Rice is a zombie and I'm not the antidote anymore, and I just almost got bitten by that weirdo, and if he had had just one tooth, I'd be a goner right now, you guys!"

"Don't worry, Madison," said Zoe, trying to comfort her friend. "Because the creepy weirdo didn't have any teeth and you're not going to turn into a zombie, okay? I promise."

"We just gotta keep going, Madison," Zack said, trying to be encouraging. "We're almost there!"

"Are we?" Madison pouted. "Because it seems like all we're doing is buying time. Face it: We're done for!"

"Madison, I know you're scared," Ozzie said. "We're all scared. But right now we all need to be tough and stick together. We're only as strong as our weakest link."

Zack looked at Rice trying to chew through the mouth hole of his gorilla mask. *Nom-nom-nom.*

He hoped Ozzie was wrong about that.

CHAPTER 11

New York City's Upper West Side was a flash of red-white-and-blue ambulance lights. Police sirens blared their shrill whoops through the crisp night air. The whole street reeked like the gunk beneath a grungy toenail. Zack almost gagged on the pungent fumes as they hurried up to street level, now dragging Rice by the leash up the staircase one step at a time. Fresh off the subway, they found themselves on a familiar block. Zack looked up and noticed that they were back at the museum where the zombie exhibit had opened earlier that morning.

"Hang on, you guys," Zack said, and raced up

the stone steps. "I'll be right back." He burst into the museum and looked around the entrance hall. Zombie moans resounded throughout the building, but Zack had a clear shot to the human brain sample, a part of the exhibit. Zack cranked back his arm and struck the display case with the butt end of his umbrella. The glass shattered to pieces and Zack picked up the human brain, then raced back outside.

Zack walked down the stone steps, holding the brain specimen in his hand.

"Ew, Zack, gross!" Madison cringed. "What's that for?"

"You know how they lead a horse by dangling a carrot in front of its face?"

"Yeah," Madison said. "I guess."

"Same idea," Zack said, digging through Rice's pack for supplies. "Except zombies don't like carrots. . . ." He tied the brain with string from the backpack to the end of one of the umbrellas and held the strung-up brain over Rice's head, keeping it just out of biting distance. "They like brains." He smiled.

Zombie Rice marched ahead, led by Zack dangling the brain in front of his face. They all crossed the street together, retracing their steps through the Central Park gates into the green oasis at the center of Manhattan. They worked their way down a dirt path winding through a patch of contorted trees twisting up out of the ground like giant hands clawing for outer space.

A patch of clouds blotted out the moon, and the night darkened, making it much harder to distinguish zombies from shadows. The park was less infested than Midtown had been, but there were still plenty of

undead city dwellers prowling through this man-made wilderness.

Zack was doing his best to lead zombie Rice quickly along the trail, but the brain was attracting some unwanted attention.

"Glyrghlphle!" Dozens of flesh-hungry lunatics stumbled down the hills and rocky slopes.

"Are you sure this was a good idea, little bro?" whispered Zoe from behind.

"Actually," Zack whisper-yelled back, "I guess I didn't really think it all the way through."

"Ahhh!" Madison shrieked as a balding zombie man with long stringy blond hair shambled onto the pathway.

"Hey!" Zack shouted, and swung the tethered brain in front of the zombie freak like a hypnotist's pocket watch. The undead creep stopped in place and grunted, his blank white eyes following the brain.

"Hi-ya!" Madison cranked back her arm and thumped the zombie on his noggin. The beast dropped to his knees and fell face-forward into the dirt.

"Come on, you two," Ozzie called back. "Keep up!"

Zack held the umbrella over Rice's head again and zombie Rice marched forward, still desperate to get at the brain. The closer Zack held the brain to Rice's face, the faster he seemed to go. Zack picked up the pace, speed-walking now, and caught up with the gang.

Madison and Zoe were tag-teaming a zombified guy in tennis shorts and a white collared shirt. Madison whipped her handbag at the zombie's legs and at the same time Zoe clobbered him in the side of the head. The undead tennis pro flipped head over heels and landed on the grass with a crunchy splat.

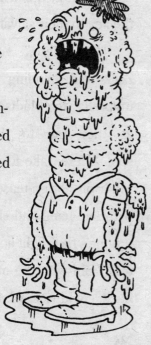

Ozzie ran up to a zombie lurching forward out of the tree-lined path. The mutant grown-up looked like a giant dweeb, with baggy khaki pants and a tucked-in polo shirt. A nasty growth of scabby boils hung off its eye cavity like a cluster of overripe grapes.

Ozzie thwacked the undead madman in the face, squashing the mass of clustered boils, which burst like a pus-filled piñata.

Zack paused, taking a second to scan the park. He kept Rice still by lifting the brain over Rice's noggin. This was the right spot, Zack thought, though the place looked different in the dark.

"Are we almost there?" asked Madison, stopping beside him.

Then Zack saw it, the trash can holding the key to their salvation.

"Over there," Zack said, handing the umbrella to Madison as they ran to the spot. "Here, take Rice." Madison brain-teased Rice with one hand and shined her iPhone's flashlight app into the trash can with the other so Zack could see what he was doing. Zack peered down into the garbage bin filled with people's disgusting trash that had piled up throughout the day. Zack reached down and riffled through the can in search of Madison's magical Band-Aid.

Zack tossed out old Chinese food containers and sticky coffee cups that stank of sour milk, but he didn't care. He was so close to getting exactly what they came for. He pulled up another handful of garbage and sifted through it— a brown-spotted banana peel and some used Kleenex.

"Yuck!" said Madison, bringing her iPhone up to her mouth to hold back her nausea. "It's not there."

"Wait. Gimme the light," said Zack, pulling out yet another handful of trash, this time a greasy paper plate from their pizza picnic earlier in the day. Stuck on the end of the plate, a lone Band-Aid hung. Zack's eyes grew wide, and he plucked it off, pinching the unzombifying bandage in front of his face like an old-school movie director looking at a strip of film. A large red dot of Madison's vegan blood stained the white pad. "I got it!" Zack shouted. "I got it!"

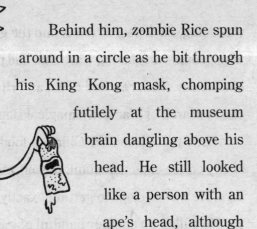

Behind him, zombie Rice spun around in a circle as he bit through his King Kong mask, chomping futilely at the museum brain dangling above his head. He still looked like a person with an ape's head, although now the gorilla had a human mouth and teeth. Rice spun and spun, making himself dizzy.

"Guys!" Zack said, and turned to show Ozzie and Zoe. "We got—"

"Rice!" Madison shouted, losing her grip on the umbrella. "Get back here!"

"Blarghle-snargle!"

Wham!

Zombie Rice bumped into Zack, gnawing blindly at the air. Completely caught off guard, Zack put up his hands to block his best friend's zombie assault. Rice's two front teeth nipped the Band-Aid from Zack's fingertips, and time slowed to a standstill.

"*Noooooooooo!*" Zack screamed, his eyes widening. He grabbed for the King Kong mask, but zombie Rice thrashed him to the ground before he could. Zack's rear end hit the damp grass as he watched his monkey-headed friend gobble up the Band-Aid.

Zack crawled over quickly and grabbed Rice by the face. "No!" he yelled. "Spit it out!"

But it was too late.

Rice had just swallowed their only hope. "*Guggh!*" Zombie Rice belched once and keeled over as his whole body fell slack in the grass.

CHAPTER 12

Wearing his night-vision goggles, Ozzie Briggs karate-chopped the last zombie in their area—an undead skater punk rocking ripped jeans and a tank top showing off his mangled, tattooed arm. The zombie's innards sloshed from the kung fu blow, and twin streams of yolky mucus shot out from both his nostrils. Ozzie dodged the slimy shrapnel and jogged over to where Zack was sitting next to Rice's now unconscious body lying in the grass. "What the— What did you do?" Ozzie asked pulling off his goggles.

Zoe came over, filling in the blanks. She pointed to her brother. "He found the Band-Aid, which was really,

really awesome, but also pretty gross. Then Rice ate the Band-Aid, which was even grosser, but not nearly as awesome."

"What the heck, man?" Ozzie yelled. "You let him eat the Band-Aid?"

"I didn't *let* him do anything," Zack said, rising to his feet. "Maybe if you weren't such a showboat, you would have been over here helping us out."

"Showboat?" Ozzie shouted, and jumped over Rice, who lay prone on the grass at their feet. "I'm the one who's been doing all the work and saving your puny butt all over town!"

"Hey," Zoe joined in the yelling. "Nobody talks to my brother like that except for *moi*. Plus, I save his butt, like, every two seconds! So don't go taking all the credit."

Twinkles walked over to Rice and lapped a globule of slime off his King Kong mask. Just then Rice's eyes snapped open, but everyone was too busy yelling to notice.

"Can we please stop bickering?" Madison said. "We're on the same team. What are we supposed to do now? That stupid Band-Aid was our only hope!"

"Guys?" Rice's voice sounded from behind the mask. "What's going on? Why am I all tied up?"

"Rice!" Zack shouted happily. "You're not a zombie anymore!" He ran over and helped his buddy to his feet.

Zoe, however, went up to Rice and whacked him upside the head. "Thanks a lot, monkey brains. Now we're all dead meat."

"Ow!" Rice yelled, grabbing his head and pulling off the mask. "What was our only hope?"

"The Band-Aid!" everyone shouted.

"What Band-Aid?"

"The one Madison had on before she ate the pizza!" Zoe shouted.

"Yo," said Rice. "How good was that pizza?"

"Yeah," said Zack. "So good it unveganized her blood."

Rice turned to look at Madison. "No way!"

"Afraid so, Ricey-poo," Madison said.

"Listen, dude," Zack said. "The popcorn antidote just all of a sudden wore off and everyone who ate it rezombified. Including you. Madison can't unzombify anything anymore, and the Band-Aid you ate was the last drop of antidote on the planet. But despite all that, it's great to have you back, even though you messed everything up. No offense."

"Well, then," said Rice. "We just gotta make a new Madison!"

"Well, that's obviously going to be impossible," Madison said. "I'm one of a kind."

"But maybe you're onto something," Zack said. "Duplessis did say we had to find more vegans."

Madison pointed to her new Bio-Wear shoes from Macy's. "Oooh, look up Bio-Wear! Their company is based in Brooklyn. They advertised that everything from the material to the employees handling the shoes were vegan. Maybe that will give us a lead."

Rice pulled out his phone, did a quick Google search, and found that Bio-Wear also owned an Organic Food Warehouse in Brooklyn that hosted a vegan meet-up group nearly every night.

"OMG," Madison said. "I've totally heard of that."

"Good call, guys," Ozzie said. "But can we continue this conversation somewhere else?" Ozzie pointed to a humongous throng of zombies moving across the park grounds. The undead creepazoids stalked through Central Park as if they were wading through a knee-deep pool of Jell-O.

"Run!" Zack shouted.

They took off into the park until Madison came to a halt. "You guys hear that?" she asked as everyone stopped alongside her.

They looked in the direction of the noise and saw a black-and-white horse attached to a carriage. The horse struggled to pull the carriage between two trees, but the big wheels were too wide to make it through. The poor horse whinnied desperately as a quartet of zombified bird-watchers staggered toward the creature. The undead bird-watchers moaned and wailed with binoculars around their putrid, flaking necks.

"Come on, guys!" Madison shouted. "We've got to save him!"

"Are you kidding me?" Rice asked.

"She's right, Rice," said Ozzie. "If we help him, we won't have to get out of the park on foot, and I can ride."

"Hurry up," Madison said. "They're going to rip out his little horsey brains!"

They all ran over to where the horse and buggy were wedged between the trees. Zoe walloped the zombie bird-watchers one at a time, while Madison and the boys guided the horse backward, dislodging the carriage from the tree trunks.

Zack, Zoe, Madison, and Rice hopped into the carriage, and Ozzie jumped up in the driver's seat with Twinkles perched anxiously on his lap.

"Giddyap!" Madison yelled.

Ozzie slapped the reins and the horse began to trot, pulling the carriage away from the zombie onrush.

As they rode in the buggy, Rice looked off into the zombified park, pinching the air in front of his eyeball. Every time his index finger touched his thumb, he made torpedo noises.

"What are you doing?" Zack said.

"I'm pretending I can crush the zombies with my fingers."

Zoe lined up Rice's head and pinched the air in front of her own eyeball. "Pow!"

"Hold on, guys!" Ozzie yelled as zombies started to stumble onto the pathway, flailing their arms at the carriage. Ozzie slapped the reins and the horse began to pick up speed.

The carriage flew along the walking path that curved around the bank of a pond. As they galloped ahead, Zack recognized one of the zombies from earlier that day. The zombie stilt walker must have been thirteen feet tall, and it was lumbering into their path.

"Watch out!" Zack yelled.

The horse and buggy were going too fast to swerve, and the undead street clown toppled into the carriage, spooking the horse. The carriage shook and bounced as the animal neighed and veered off the path full steam ahead toward the pond. Ozzie tightened the reins to steer the horse back on track, but just then one of the zombie clown's long wooden stilts slipped between the spokes in the wheel of the carriage.

The buggy flipped and sent them all spinning

through the air in what seemed like slow motion. Zack opened his eyes mid-somersault and caught a clear view of the moon, now free of the clouds, hanging low in the starry sky. Before he could look anywhere else, Zack belly-flopped into the pond with Rice screaming, "Cowabunga!"

Kersplash! Madison and Zoe both cannonballed into the water with a double plunk, and the undead stilt-walking clown plunked into the water after them.

Zack rose out of the rippling water, gasping for air. He was drenched and covered in green algae. Madison and Zoe brushed pond scum out of their hair.

As they waded back to dry land, Rice did a quick head count. "Where's Ozzie?"

Zack pointed across the green to the detached horse galloping away from the wreckage of the carriage. Ozzie was nowhere to be seen.

"OMG!" Madison gasped. "Twinkles! Where's Twinkles!"

"Tween-kles!" Rice called. "Ozz-eee!" He looked down at his shoeless foot. "Hey! What happened to my sneaker?"

Zack looked down at his mismatched footwear. "Sorry, man. You owed me one."

The Central Park riffraff prowled along the greens, swarms and swarms of zombie creeps teetering toward them in an unrelenting torrent of tooth and claw.

There was nowhere to hide. They had to get out of the park, with or without Ozzie and Twinkles.

CHAPTER 13

Zack, Madison, Zoe, and Rice jogged down a dark side street on the Upper East Side, soaking wet from the pond in Central Park.

Brownstones and tenements lined both sides of the block. The fire escapes on the front of the apartment buildings looked like Zs stacked on top of one another.

"We have to find Twinkles," Madison said, her puppy-dog eyes welling up with tears.

"More important," said Rice, "we've got to find Ozzie. There's no way we're leaving him!"

"But first," Zack called to them, "we need to find some wheels. . . ."

A short way down the next block they spotted a row of unchained bicycles belonging to a crew of zombified food delivery guys. The undead delivery dudes crisscrossed, tottering slantwise around their bikes. As Rice and the girls scoped out their wheels, Zack locked eyes with one of the zombie brutes, who grunted and licked his gangrenous chops. All at once, three of his rezombified buddies turned, casting their dead-eyed gazes on their brain-nuggety prey. The undead clan of bike messengers lurched slowly toward them. Something foul oozed from one of their eye sockets like egg yolk.

"Okay, guys, one, two, three!" Zack, Rice, Zoe, and Madison bum-rushed the zombified delivery guys.

Zack swung a surviving umbrella and hooked a lanky zombie by the neck. He followed through and the undead beast slammed to the ground with a dull splat. Rice ran behind the zombified goon with the dribbling eyeball and crouched behind his knees. Madison sprinted and lowered her shoulder into the zombie's waist. The undead brain glutton tripped over Rice and hit the cement hard with the back of his skull. Zoe took a run and knocked out the remaining two of the mutant chowhounds with a jab-hook combo. The flesh-eating hellions tottered, swaying slightly before they both dropped to the pavement.

"I don't want to toot my own horn," Zoe said, making a muscle and kissing her biceps, "but I'm really good at this."

Zack rolled his eyes and snagged a delivery bike, then took off, worming his way through the Big Apple.

"Ozzie!" Rice and Zack chanted as they weaved in and out of zombie foot traffic. "Ozz-eeee!"

"Twinkles!" Madison shouted, her voice trembling with worry. "Twinkles!"

But all they heard were the undead moans

reverberating across Manhattan.

Zack rode behind the other three, following their lead as they turned a corner and disappeared down another street. Zack had just steered his handlebars to make the turn when his front tire hit a patch of slime. "Ahhhh!" Zack cried as the bike skidded out of control.

He crashed into a street lamp and hit the deck hard, falling facedown in a sewer grate. He scrambled to his feet and wiped the zombie sludge off his hands. He looked all around, but Rice, Zoe, and Madison were nowhere in sight. A harsh wind blew debris along the sidewalk, sending ripples through the puddles of sludge gathered along the curb. The street lamps flickered like giant lightning bugs. Thick white steam rose up from a nearby manhole cover like the contrails of an evil spirit. The foggy steam switched color—red to green—under the glow of the changing traffic lights.

Zack ran over to grab the bicycle that he'd crashed onto the sidewalk, but just then a zombie horde staggered out of the fog. There were middle-aged women wearing fur coats and pearls, followed closely by their zombified husbands dressed in black tie. The upper-class horde trampled over the bicycle and backed Zack up against a restaurant on the west side of the street.

"Help!" Zack yelled, retreating under the awning of the outdoor seating area.

Zack looked over his shoulder into the dining room of the bistro. A zombie yuppie couple sat calmly at a candlelit table, getting served two entrées of brains mignon, medium-rare, by an undead waiter. The zombie couple dug into their brain filets.

The swarm of zombified well-to-doers continued to close in on Zack, dragging their feet and howling for brains. Zack looked around for some kind of defense and snatched a chair from the outside seating area. He held the chair up like a lion tamer at a circus, wooden legs pointing toward the zombies.

As he faced the oncoming swarm, a high-class zombie housewife rushed forward to the front of the pack. Zack thrust the chair and whacked the beast square in the head. The undead freak dropped to the pavement.

"That's right," Zack shouted. "Who wants some?"

The ghoulish zombies barked and snarled, all stepping forward at the same time. They thought he meant who wanted brains. *Uh-oh*, Zack thought, wishing more than anything that he had some of Ozzie's patented kung fu hustle.

Then, all of a sudden, the thick mob of undead brain munchers parted as a yellow taxicab plowed through. The taxi cleared a path to the street, then screeched to a halt. The driver stuck his head out the window. Ozzie Briggs flashed a big smile behind the wheel of the taxicab. "What are you waiting for?" Ozzie said. "Hop in!"

Zack didn't need an invitation. He was already sprinting full steam through the pathway of fallen zombies. But as Zack reached for the passenger door handle, the taxicab jolted forward and slammed to a halt, leaving him a foot behind. Zack made a face at Ozzie and reached for the handle another time. The cab jumped forward again, Ozzie giggling in the driver's seat.

"Dude!" Zack shouted, totally annoyed. "Knock it off!" He reached for the handle a third time as the zombie freaks started to lumber up behind him. The car remained still. He jumped into the passenger seat and Ozzie hit the gas.

"Very funny," Zack said with a sneer.

"Sorry, I couldn't resist," Ozzie said. "You okay?"

"Yeah," said Zack, wiping a blob of zombie slime on his pant leg. "I'm good."

"Where'd everyone else go?"

Zack looked out the window. "I lost them down that street up ahead."

"Let's go get them!"

"Arf-arf!" Twinkles barked from the backseat. The two boys and their little dog screeched off into the zombie night.

Two blocks later, they saw three figures on bicycles, pedaling like mad. Madison, Zoe, and Rice came into view.

"Why are they in such a hurry?" Ozzie said. "There aren't that many zombies here."

Looking out the windshield, Zack saw why his friends were pedaling as if their lives depended on it. A herd of New York sewer rats raced after them, nipping at their back tires. The zombie rats were as big as house cats, and fast, too.

Zack stuck his head out the window. "Come on, guys, hurry up!"

Madison, Zoe, and Rice ditched their

bikes as the yellow taxicab approached. The zombie rats blanketed the street underneath the car.

"Dude," said Rice as they hopped in and slammed the door shut. "That was a close one!"

"Ozzie!" Zoe exclaimed. "You're alive! We totally thought you were zombified."

"Ruff!" Twinkles barked, jumping onto Madison's lap.

"Twinkles!" Madison cried happily, petting her pup.

"Buckle up, guys. Time to get off this crazy island!" Ozzie said, and floored the gas pedal. The engine vroomed. The back tires spun and screeched, and a strong whiff of burned rubber seeped into the car.

"Watch out, Brooklyn." Rice yipped with excitement. "Here we come!"

The taxi sped off down the street and they were off to crash the vegan meet-up.

Hopefully, Zack thought, they weren't already too late.

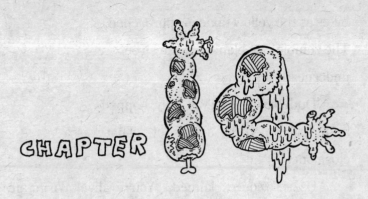

s the yellow taxi shuttled down the FDR Drive, a thick dome of gray clouds cast a dark pall over the city. Zack gazed out the window, looking westward toward the center of Manhattan. The Empire State Building glowed bright green that night. The long, thin spire sticking up from the top of the building made the skyscraper look like an enormous hypodermic syringe injecting the clouds above with its lime-colored zombie venom.

As they approached the Brooklyn Bridge, the cab suddenly slowed. The bridge was clear of traffic, but the roadway teemed with a humongous herd of gangrenous brain gluttons marching slug-gishly toward their car. At the head of the pack, a gigantic physical specimen came into focus. The shirtless zombie bodybuilder had a neck as thick as a tree trunk and wore nothing but cross-trainers and a flimsy pair of gym shorts. A road map of pulsating veins branched off from his hulk-ing square shoulders, down around his mas-sive biceps, and spiraled around his rib cage.

"Wow," Zoe said. "That zombie's in really good shape!"

"I know, right?" Madison said. "I wonder what he benches?"

The undead meathead lumbered forward out of the crowd and let out a feral yowl.

"Step on it, Oz!" yelled Rice, dismissing the girls' idle chitchat.

Madison reached over the backseat and put her hand on Ozzie's shoulder. "No way, José!"

"Ozzie, you can't be serious," Zoe said. "Turn this thing around."

"And drive back into zombie island?" Ozzie scoffed. "No, thank you very much!"

"We'll never make it across!" Madison yelled. "Not without killing some of them."

"Put it to a vote," Rice said. "All in favor say aye."

"Aye!" Zack and Ozzie both said, raising their hands along with Rice.

"Three against two!" Rice said happily. "Hit the gas, Oz!"

Twinkles pawed the window and glanced out at the zombie march. "Arf!" the puppy barked, and then cowered back down in Madison's lap.

"Ha!" said Zoe. "That was a 'no'! Three to three. It's a tie. Now turn around!"

"Twinkles's vote doesn't count," said Rice. "He's

just a pea-brained little dog!"

"You're just a pea-brained little dog!" Madison yelled.

"That doesn't even make sense, Madison," Rice fired back. "There's nothing canine about me."

"Hey!" Zack yelled. "There's not going to be anything human about us either if we don't get across this bridge."

"Time to put the pedal to the metal, ladies." Ozzie smiled in the rearview and revved the engine.

"Whatever," the girls both said, fastening their seat belts tighter.

"Just don't get us killed, okay, Mr. Hotshot?" Zoe said, glaring at Ozzie.

"Uh-oh," Ozzie said, shifting out of park and locking the car doors.

"What-oh?" asked Zack, peering out ahead of them.

Suddenly, the rezombified bodybuilder ran toward the taxi and slammed into the hood with a bang.

Ozzie hit the gas, but the slime-soaked zombie horde made it impossible to accelerate and they slowed to a crawl. The yellow taxi coasted through the undead mob like a funhouse roller coaster.

"Holy snap!" Rice screamed as the muscle-bound zombie climbed up the hood and onto the windshield of the moving car. The beast's well-toned abdominals pressed against the windshield. The zombie's six-pack burbled and pulsed with crops of pustules bulging off his skin, and its red sinewy muscles peeked out from various open sores where the flesh had begun to rot away.

"Ew, gnarly!" Madison cringed, covering her eyes and Twinkles's, too.

The decomposing muscleman cranked his arm back and blasted his fist clear through the windshield on the driver's side.

The zombie's forearm reached in and groped around, trying to palm Ozzie's face like a basketball. Dark brown slime oozed from its stretched-open hand and gave off a stench like a Porta Potty at a state fair.

At the same time, the windows were getting a zombie car wash as slimy arms slapped against the side of the cab and undead fish faces pressed up against the glass. The undead swarm was starting to

cover the taxi like a mass of bees on a honeycomb.

"I can't see anything!" Ozzie said, dodging the zombie's putrid hand and steering the car steadily through the multitude of tottering ghouls. "Zack, you gotta drive, man, while I get rid of this guy."

"Huh?" Zack didn't have time to protest. He leaned over and took the wheel, then reached his foot over and placed it on the gas pedal as Ozzie took his off. Ozzie rolled down his window and stood up in the driver's seat. Holding his nunchakus in his left hand, he reached out of the taxi and bopped the undead bodybuilder repeatedly, but the hardheaded lunatic would not budge.

Inside, the psychotic muscleman's hand was still stuck through the windshield. Zack steered their zombie-covered cab onward across the bridge through the brain-hungry horde.

Outside, a zombie reached out of the mob and snatched at Ozzie's shirtsleeve. *"Rargh!"* With one swift elbow to the schnoz, Ozzie sent the zombie heathen screeching back into the swarm.

"Time for plan B!" Ozzie said, hopping back inside

on the glass-strewn seat cushion and taking control of the car from Zack. He sped up a little and then slammed on the brakes hard. *Uhrrk!* They all jolted forward in their seats as the muscle-bound freakazoid flew off the hood of the taxi onto the shoulder.

"See ya," Ozzie shouted. "Wouldn't want to be ya!" He hit the gas pedal and they shot through the zombie clearing.

But the sudden stop did more than knock the zombie off. It also severed its arm at the elbow. The dismembered forearm dropped to the floor inside the car and scurried under the seat like a frightened animal.

The zombie forearm scampered out from under the passenger's seat and into the back with Rice and the girls. It shot straight up from the floor, making a duck-bill with its four fingers and thumb, and swayed back and forth like a king cobra about to strike.

Madison and Zoe let out twin screams of terror, and the rear windshield popped from the sonic force of their shrill shrieking.

"Calm down," Rice said in a soothing voice. "He's

way more scared of us than we are of him. . . ." He held out his hand as if he were letting a dog sniff his scent. Then he tried to catch the loose arm, but the undead appendage disappeared down by their feet.

"OMG, OMG," Madison cried. "Where'd it go?"

"It's under Ozzie's seat!"

"Whoa!" Ozzie shouted, and all of a sudden the car jumped forward. The severed arm had grabbed Ozzie by the ankle and was jamming his foot down hard on the accelerator. The taxi swerved ahead and zoomed past the last remaining zombies on the bridge.

"Ozzie, slow down!" Madison yelled.

"I can't!"

Zack leaned over toward the driver's seat, trying to pry his fingers under the renegade forearm's digits and loosen its zombie grip on Ozzie's leg.

"Almost got it," Zack said, working his middle and index finger around the thing's thumb. "There!" He yanked as hard as he could and the zombie forearm released its grip. Zack grabbed the arm with both hands, one on the thumb, the other on the pinkie, and tossed it out the window. The zombified forearm flew back behind the car and vanished for good.

"Ozzie, if we don't slow down, we're gonna crash!" Madison yelled.

Ozzie slammed the brakes and spun the steering wheel, but they were flying out of control. "Hold on!" Ozzie shouted.

Zack closed his eyes, preparing for the worst, when he heard the tires screech to a halt.

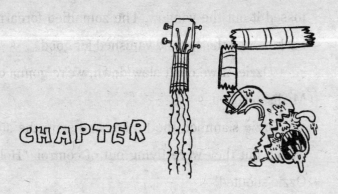

CHAPTER 15

Everyone jerked forward in their seats except for Twinkles, who flew through the windowless windshield and landed on the grass on the side of the roadway.

"You guys okay?" Zack asked, scrunched on the floor in front of the passenger seat.

"Yup," Rice said. "I'm good."

"Uh-huh." Madison and Zoe both nodded their heads. Madison opened the side door for Twinkles, who jumped back inside the car.

"Arf-arf!" Twinkles was okay, too.

Ozzie eased the busted-up taxicab back in

gear and drove off through the streets. The engine squeaked and rattled with every turn, and as their car trundled off into Brooklyn, Zack watched the New York skyline slowly disappear in his side-view mirror.

A few blocks down, with no zombies in sight, Ozzie pressed the brakes and they squeaked to a stop at a four-way intersection.

"Okay, Rice," said Zack. "Which way do we go?"

"Hold on one sec," said Rice, looking down at his smartphone. "My 4G's taking for-ever. . . ."

As Rice Googled directions, zombified Brooklynites started appearing on the fringes of the street. They lurked out of the shadows, staggering slowly from the alleyways and demolished storefront windows. They limped toward the yellow taxi, which was stopped under the traffic lights flashing green, then yellow, then red.

"Ozzie, let's go already," Madison said. "Come on!"

"Yeah," Zoe said. "These guys look like they're ready for a midnight snack."

"I'm trying," said Ozzie, stepping on the gas pedal. "It's not going!"

"Turn it on again," Rice suggested. "Maybe we just stalled out."

Ozzie turned the ignition key over, but the engine

coughed and wheezed a noise that sounded like an electric pencil sharpener before falling silent. Their getaway car was dead. The undead clamor rose up all around them, a symphony of glurping moans and murmuring wails like Halloween sound effects.

The zombie throng gathered around them in a shrinking semicircle of ravenous faces clacking their teeth compulsively.

"We gotta make a run for it!" Madison grabbed Twinkles and stuffed him in her bag. The five of them threw open the cab doors and ditched their ride, running away from the mutant horde shambling toward them.

"Rice!" yelled Zack, as they hustled down the street and came to another intersection. "We need directions, man. Left or right?"

Rice jogged behind them, bringing up the rear as he studied the map on his phone. "Right!" he called. "If we cut through the park, we'll be able to stay off the streets and be there in half the time. Come on!"

They all hung a right down the zombified street

hell-bordered with brain-craving crazies. Zack led the charge and took a running jump over a small bush as they booked across a grassy lawn toward a thicket of trees. The Brooklyn zombie foot traffic listed to the left and swayed to the right as they trailed Zack, Rice, Madison, Ozzie, and Zoe into Prospect Park.

"Keep moving, guys!" Rice shouted as he sprinted with his smartphone, bringing up the rear. "Just a little bit farther!"

Zack clutched his umbrella, ready for war, as the five of them fled into a thicket of trees at the center of the park.

As they dodged and weaved through the tree trunks, a pale white zombie man with a scraggly blond beard hobbled toward them through the dark woods, emitting a continuous choking noise, as if he had just swallowed his own tongue. He was dressed in old ratty clothes, and a snake's nest of braided dread-locks sat atop his head. He was so covered in grime and pus that he looked more like a swamp creature than anything else. His teeth protruded off his gums at unnatural angles, like the spiked inner mouth of a horror movie alien.

The undead albino man dived as the kids shot through the forest. His outstretched arm caught Zoe by the ankle and she screamed bloody murder, stuck with one foot wrapped up in the zombie's tight clutch.

"Zack!" she shouted for her brother, and he stopped in his tracks.

Zack bolted over to his sister while she struggled to kick free from the zombie beast clawing her ankle. Another zombie popped out from the darkness, a five-foot-tall young zombie woman with short-cropped blond hair and a guitar case slung over her shoulder.

Zack sprinted toward the zombie guitarist chick and sidestepped around the back of her, catching the latches of the guitar case with his fingertips. He flicked it open, and the zombie girl's acoustic guitar fell to the ground. Zack picked it up in a flash, raised it over his head, and smashed it down on its owner's undead noggin.

Bloomph!

The zombie spun around, thrashing and flailing. With her head still inside the splintered instrument, she dropped to the ground in a heap.

Zack turned and lined up the albino zombie swamp creature, toe-blasting him in the face with a soccer kick from Rice's sneaker. The zombie man yowled hideously, letting go of its grip around Zoe's leg.

"Thanks, bro!" said Zoe as she and Zack sprinted double-time into the woods to catch up with Ozzie, Madison, and Rice.

As they did, Madison let out a bloodcurdling scream and skidded to a halt. "Guys!" she cried. "Wait!"

Zack stopped running and looked over at Madison, who was staring petrified at two shadowy figures— a man and a woman—traipsing into the park forest up ahead.

"What's the matter, Madison?" Ozzie called over to her. "It's just a couple of zombies. . . ."

"Nuh-uh!" Zoe shook her head, standing next to her BFF.

The shadowy undead figures were not alone. Zack squinted through the darkness. Two wild swarms of zombified animals swirled about the rezombified man and woman. A flock of squawking zombie pigeons flapped around the ferocious flesh-guzzling man, while a pack of rabid squirrels spiraled up the legs and torso of the rezombified woman. There were dozens if not hundreds of the wretched little creatures roiling all around the rancorous animal hoarders.

Zoe let out a loud involuntary shriek cut short by Rice's hand clamping around her mouth.

"Shhhh!" Rice shushed her.

Zoe spit Rice's unrezombified hand out of her mouth and gagged. "Eww!" she whispered. "You taste like rotten pepperoni!"

The squirrel lady's fluffy-tailed zombie critters zeroed in on them with their bug-eyed gazes, their all-sensing noses sniffing out human brains like trained bloodhounds tracking a wounded animal through the forest.

This is not good, Zack thought. *If any one of those things catches a nibble of Madison or Ozzie, they'll turn into zombies like that!* He turned to Madison and Ozzie. "You two need to get out of here!"

"What?" Madison said.

"Me, Zoe, and Rice will lure those things that way," he said.

"We will?" Rice asked incredulously.

"Did you lose your mind or something, little bro?" Zoe said.

"We can't risk either of them getting bitten by one of those things," Zack explained. "But if the three of us get bitten, then it doesn't matter. We'll still stay human."

"He's right, Madison," Ozzie said, grabbing her by the arm. "You guys, take those things that way. We'll go around the other way and meet back up with you at the vegan warehouse."

Rice showed Ozzie the map of the neighborhood on his smartphone.

"Got it!" Ozzie said, giving the thumbs-up, and

he and Madison raced off in the opposite direction. Zoe and the boys then started shouting, diverting the squirrel lady's and pigeon man's attentions away from their friends,

"Over here, Squirrel Lady!" Rice shouted as he jumped up and down, waving his hands in the air. The hoard of undead squirrels skittered around the zombie man's ankles. Pigeon Man snarled, leading his pack like some psychotic pied piper of Brooklyn.

"Hey!" Zoe shouted. "Squirrel Lady! This way!"

Squirrel Lady's head whipped around at the sound of Zoe's voice. "Raaaargh!" The undead animal hoarder lifted her mangled arms and moaned, walking straight for them. The man's flock of zombie pigeons launched off the ground, flapping their undead wings laboriously, flying slowly, as if they were carrying invisible bricks with their talons.

"Run!" Zack shouted, and bolted into a sprint as the birds flew at them.

Rice and Zoe took off, the herd of zombie squirrels chasing them through the trees.

"Zack," yelled Zoe to her brother. "This was your worst idea ever!"

As they raced through the park, the twin swarms of undead animals were gaining ground. The squirrels were right on their heels, and the pigeons lumbered through the night air, catching up fast.

All of a sudden, Zoe tripped in a ditch and fell in the dirt. "Ahhhh!" she cried as a trio of zombie pigeons descended on her head.

"Cover your eyes," Rice yelled, doubling back to help her.

Zack ran back, too, and together they batted the pigeons off Zoe's head and hoisted her back up to her feet.

Just then the herd of zombie squirrels caught up with them and pounced. Zack quickly opened the umbrella and blocked the undead fuzzballs with the tented nylon fabric, deflecting a dozen fluffy-tailed critters to the ground. But that wasn't the last of them. Another squirrel immediately scurried up the outside of his leg. The little sucker's teeth stung as they bit into Zack's flesh through his pants.

Rice ran over and snatched the feasting squirrel by its bushy tail. He ripped the undead rodent off his buddy's thigh and flipped it up in the air. Rice then bobbed in place like a heavyweight boxer and nailed the little sucker with a right cross. The zombie squirrel squealed and sailed into a tree trunk with a vicious splat.

"Good one, Rice," said Zack, clutching his pant leg.

They squinted through the darkness and saw the

moonlight hitting the grass just beyond the edge of the woods.

"Come on!" Zoe shouted.

And with hundreds of undead hellhounds waddling behind them through the urban woodland, the three of them dashed out of the zombified forest.

CHAPTER  **16**

Zack, Zoe, and Rice stopped in the small parking lot outside the Organic Food Warehouse, grabbing their knees and sucking in air. "This is the place." Rice gasped, looking up from his iPhone at the large food depot.

"Where are Ozzie and Madison?" asked Zoe, wheezing a bit, too.

"They're probably inside," Zack said.

They pushed through the doors and discovered the whole place was dark and quiet. Rice pulled out a flashlight from his backpack and flipped it on, shining the beam of light around the room. The vegan food warehouse had twenty-foot ceilings, and huge shelving units towered from the ground up.

"Madison!" Zoe called.

"Shhhh!" Zack said. "There could be zombies in here for all we know. . . ."

"Ozzie!" Rice whispered into the creepy, deserted food warehouse.

"Where are they?" asked Zoe, sounding a little worried.

"I don't know. They had a good head start," Zack said. "They should be here by now."

"Maybe they got lost," Zoe said. "We should go look for them."

"Hey, guys," said Rice, going down one of the food aisles. "Check it out."

"Do you see them?" Zack asked.

"No," Rice said. "But I found something else." He was standing in front of a gigantic stack of Madison's favorite drink: kiwi-strawberry ginkgo biloba–infused Vital Vegan PowerPunch. "We gotta stock up on this stuff! Once we find a pure vegan, we can have them

drink Vital Vegan and re-Madison them. And boom—
more antidote!"

"Are you sure that will work?" Zoe asked skeptically.

"Of course it'll work," said Rice. "It worked with
Madison, didn't it?"

"Well, let's load up then," Zack said, picking up a
case of the Vital Vegan drink.

As they made their stack of the ginkgo vitamin
water, Rice's phone started to ring. He looked at the touch

screen flashing an unknown number. He answered the call: "Hello?"

"Rice!" cried the voice on the other end of the line. "It's Ozzie."

"Yo, Oz! What's up? Where are you guys?"

"Is Madison okay?" Zoe asked.

"Hey," Rice said into the phone. "Is Madison all right?"

"Yeah," Ozzie said. "She's fine, and so is Twinkles."

"Where are you?" Rice asked Ozzie.

"We're across the street at the botanical gardens," he said. "No zombies over here. Where are you three?"

"We're at the warehouse still," Rice said.

"Well, get your butts over here," Madison said in the background of the call. "We got ourselves a real live vegan dude."

"Cool," Rice said. "We've got some good news, too. We hit the jackpot on some Vital Vegan PowerPunch!"

"Great," Ozzie said. "See you soon."

Rice hung up the phone and looked at Zack and Zoe. "They found a vegan dude who can help us!"

"Come on," Zack said. "Help me load this stuff up, and let's get out of here."

"Seriously," said Zoe. "This place gives me the creeps."

"I'll be back in a second," said Zack, dropping a case of the ginkgo water on the floor. "I think I saw some of those rolly things back there." He ran to the front of the warehouse and spotted a two-wheeled dolly over by the wall next to the shopping carts. He grabbed the push-cart and scooted it to the Vital Vegan aisle.

"Better get over here, little bro," Zoe said, as Zack returned. "Something's wrong with your boy."

Zack looked up and dropped the dolly, running the rest of the way down the aisle to where his sister stood. Rice's body twitched on the floor.

"He just started doing that," Zoe said, shrugging. "Do you think he's rerezombifying?"

"And you just stood there? Rice!" Zack yelled, as he crouched down next to his pal and propped him up in his arms. "Rice!" he shouted, tapping his cheek lightly. "This isn't happening . . . no, no, no. . . ."

Just then, Rice's eyes popped open and he smiled up at Zack. "Gotcha!"

"Ha!" Zoe burst out laughing. "What a chump!"

Rice hopped off the floor and stepped to Zoe. "You owe me five bucks!"

Zack stood up and stared at the two of them. "There's something seriously wrong with both of you."

"I didn't want to, Zack," said Rice. "But, I mean . . . five bucks!"

"Come on," Zack said, shaking his head. "Go grab the dolly and let's get out of here."

Zoe wheeled the cases of ginkgo water out the back exit of the deserted organic warehouse, and they followed Rice's iPhone directions to the botanical gardens. "Almost there? I thought it was across the street?" Zack asked, as they made their way down a few more twists and turns.

"Not almost," said Rice. "We're here."

CHAPTER

Outside the giant greenhouselike structure, Zoe and the boys passed a food truck parked out front. The words 100% VEGAN CUISINE labeled the side of the vehicle. They walked through the halls of the glass building until they reached a large room with all sorts of rare and beautiful flowers. Toward the back of the room, they saw Madison, Ozzie, and a young man who was sitting on the ground in yoga position with his legs crossed. His hands rested on his knees, making "okay" signs with his fingertips.

Zack raised his eyebrows at the meditating vegan. "Is he okay?"

"Yeah," Madison said. "Apparently he does this a lot."

"He claims to be warding off the dark spirits of zombieism," Ozzie said.

Is this dude for real? Zack thought, propping the stack of ginkgo water against the glass wall.

"Welcome . . ." The man's voice resounded through the greenhouse. "Come, friends. Join me."

"This guy is going to be perfect." Rice smiled. "What's his deal?"

"His name is Egon Furlong," Ozzie informed them. "He's a hundred percent pure vegan, and he drives that food truck parked out front."

"I see you've brought me a tasty libation," said Egon the vegan, eyeing the dolly full of vitamin water. "Kiwi-strawberry is one of my favorite flavors the Vital

Vegan brand has to offer."

"Hey," Madison said. "Me, too!"

"Great minds drink alike."

"Boo!" said Zoe. "Dad joke!"

Ozzie elbowed Zoe in the ribs. "Don't make fun of him," he whispered. "We need his help, remember?"

Zack and Rice took a seat next to the last of the vegans and crossed their legs.

"So," Zack said. "You've never been a zombie before?"

"No," he said. "I managed to survive the last out-break. Luckily, I was meditating at my cabin in the mountains and there were no zombies for miles."

"That's good," Rice said. "So would you be willing to help us produce a new antidote?"

"You believe that I might produce some of the same vegan powers that your friend once possessed?"

He gestured toward Madison. "And unzombify the population?"

"Yes," Zack said sincerely. "We do." *Let's hope he drinks as much of the Vital Vegan punch as Madison does,* Zack thought.

There was a moment of silence while Egon pondered the invitation. "Then that will be my destiny."

"Awesome," Ozzie said, ripping open one of the cases of Vital Vegan. "Here," he said. "Take this." He handed Egon a bottle of the kiwi-strawberry drink.

The man sipped the ginkgo water and smacked his lips. "Mm-hmm, that is a tasty beverage!"

It was actually kind of peaceful in the greenhouse. They all caught their breath as Egon drank the Vital Vegan, forgetting for a moment about the zombie-pocalypse going on.

Zack yawned loudly, only just realizing how tired he was after their night of fighting through the zombie hordes.

"Quit yawning, Zack," said Zoe. "You're making me sleepy."

"Maybe if we take turns keeping watch, we can all get a little shut-eye," said Rice.

It seemed like a great idea, until a horrible zombie howl echoed from outside. The zombie battle cry shattered their hope of sleep, and they all realized at once that any kind of rest might still be a long way off.

All of a sudden another sound erupted, this time even closer. It was the sound of breaking glass.

"Run!" Zack shouted, as the glass panels started to crack with the hundredfold zombie onslaught smashing outside.

Egon scrambled off the floor and shot out through the greenhouse garden.

"Over there!" Madison signaled to the back corner of the greenhouse, away from the herd of undead creeps.

Ozzie jogged over and grabbed the cart full of ginkgo biloba water, then took off after the girls.

Zack and Rice raced through the maze of exotic plants, trailing their new vegan guru. As they hustled down the walkway, Rice's eyes went wide. "Egon," he screamed. "Watch out!"

Zack looked in front of them and saw a zombified Venus flytrap lash out like a serpent.

Ahead of them, Egon fell to his knees, clutching his wrist. "Owwww!" The last of the vegans bellowed in agony. Zack's stomach sank for the millionth time that night as their only hope collapsed in a heap on the floor.

"Let's get out of here!" Madison called. "I'm pretty sure zombies don't keep vegan!"

"Blargh!" the zombie vegan growled hideously, snatching at Zack's legs.

As Egon lurched off the ground, Rice stepped up from behind Zack and kicked the carnivorous vegan in the chest with the heel of his lone shoe. "Boo-ya!" Rice shouted as the zombie's head snapped back and slammed unconscious against the floor.

"Nice one, man." Zack smiled and bumped his fist with Rice's.

Just then the whole building started to rain down in shards of glass. "Shake a leg, boys!" Ozzie yelled. He raised his nunchaku and smashed an exit for them.

Zack and Rice darted over to the hole and rushed out after Ozzie and the girls as the entire greenhouse collapsed in on itself with a terrific crash.

CHAPTER

Outside, Zack flung open the back doors to Egon's vegan food truck.

Zoe hopped in the driver's seat and turned the keys still in the ignition, revving the engine. Madison and Twinkles jumped in, riding shotgun, while Zack, Ozzie, and Rice quickly loaded up their getaway truck with the cases of Vital Vegan PowerPunch.

From the shattered greenhouse, psychotic glass-speckled zombies sparkled in the streetlight and shambled after them with thick pus oozing from their lacerations.

"Let's hit the road!" said Zoe as she threw the gear-shift in reverse and peeled out into the street, screeching away from the undead madness in their wake.

"You all right, dude?" Zack asked Ozzie. "You're bleeding."

Ozzie turned his head to see the rip in the back of his shirtsleeve. "Just a scrape. No biggie."

"Hey," Rice said to Zack, "you're bleeding, too."

Zack looked down at the bloody spot on his pant leg and picked a tiny tooth out of the cut in his leg. "Just a zombie squirrel bite." He smiled, tossing away the tooth. "No biggie."

Rice unzipped his pack and pulled out some first-aid supplies, along with an assortment of individually wrapped snack cakes. "Don't leave home without 'em."

But then, as the excitement from their brush with the undead waned, a solemn mood washed over their ride.

"So what are we going to do now?" Zack asked. "All we have is a bunch of kiwi-strawberry vitamin water."

Rice pounded his fist against the inside of the truck. "If only they had cloned Madison when they had the chance . . . ," he said, trailing off.

"Come on, Rice," Ozzie said. "Let's not play the 'what if' game. We gotta stay focused."

"You're right, Oz," Rice said, taking a deep breath. "What the heck do we do now?" The five of them sat quietly for a few moments before Madison broke the silence.

"OMG!" Her eyes lit up with a bright idea. "I can't believe I didn't think of it till now," she said, perking up a bit. "My cousin Olivia . . . she's, like, totally my clone. She's on the same diet as me and everything. We, like, totally look the same, too, except she's got brown hair and I'm a little prettier."

"Hmm." Rice scratched his chin. "Interesting."

"That's it," Zack agreed. "We've gotta get to her right away."

"Okay, so where am I driving to, guys?" asked Zoe.

"Umm, it's kind of far," Madison replied. "She's Canadian, but she lives right across the border near Niagara Falls."

"What do you say, guys," Ozzie said, as they drove deeper into Brooklyn. "You down for another road trip?"

"Whatever it takes, man," Zack said, feeling slightly better. "Whatever it takes. . . ."

"All in favor say 'eyeballs,'" Rice said.

"Eyeballs!" the five of them said together.

"Arf!" Twinkles barked. "Arf-arf!"

"Canada, here we come!" said Zoe, whooping. She pulled the truck onto the highway and they zoomed off to track down Madison's cousin and unzombify the world.

Again.

What cranium-craving cretins will
the Zombie Chasers battle next?

Read a sneak peek of the
next **ZOMBIE CHASERS** novel,

The windshield wipers clacked hypnotically back and forth as the vegan food truck sped along the frozen lakeshore toward Buffalo, New York. Zack Clarke sat and watched the snowflakes fall in the fading twilight. The entire area was still in the dead of winter, despite the spring weather elsewhere.

Behind the wheel, Ozzie Briggs followed a detour sign and steered the truck off the expressway into the city.

It had been almost ten hours since they had escaped a rezombified New York City. Now they were on a mission to track down Madison's vegan cousin, Olivia, the one person who could help them formulate another zombie antidote.

Madison sat in the back, her cell phone pressed to her ear, trying to reach her cousin. "It's going straight to voice mail," she whined.

"At least we have her address," Rice piped in.

Ozzie slowed the food truck at a blinking yellow traffic light. In front of them, the road turned into a circular roundabout with a large white obelisk jutting out of the center.

All of a sudden—*Bam! Bam! Bam!*

"We've got company!" Zack glimpsed back in the side-view mirror. Two undead figures latched tightly to the exterior panel of the truck. The zombies, a man wearing boxer shorts and a black puffy vest and a woman in a bathrobe and pink bunny slippers, looked as though they had rezombified in the middle of getting dressed. A mustache of snot rimed across the undead bathrobe lady's upper lip, which curled back to show off her purplish, bloodstained teeth.

"Buckle your seat belts, guys!" Ozzie swerved the food truck from side to side, attempting to shake the undead joyriders loose.

"The zombies aren't coming off," Zack said. "They're stuck!"

"What do you mean they're stuck?" Madison asked.

"I mean stuck," Zack said. "Like that kid's tongue that touched the flagpole in that Christmas movie kind of stuck."

"Oh, no," Ozzie muttered. "Not good."

"What's wrong?" Zack asked, turning his attention back to Ozzie.

"We're not stopping!" Ozzie shouted as the vegan food truck slid wildly on a patch of black ice. "Hold on!"

Zack stiffened in his seat as they glided toward the massive cement staircase at the foot of city hall. Ozzie spun the wheel as they swerved a hundred-eighty degrees and then jumped the curb with a loud thump.

Zack heard the two zombies detach from the side of

the truck with a sound like Velcro ripping. The undead couple rose to their feet and tottered toward them again, pawing the air, their arms red and raw from where their skin had adhered to the freezing metal.

"Go!" Zack shouted, but when Ozzie pressed the accelerator, the back wheels just spun in place.

More undead snow dwellers appeared on the staircase and began to wobble in the truck's direction.

Ozzie floored the pedal again, but the truck still wouldn't budge.

"We're caught on something!" Ozzie yelled. He looked at Zack then at Rice. "You two gotta go out there and get us unstuck."

"Fine," Rice said. "But only if you let me use your nunchacku."

Ozzie grunted.

"Please!" Rice begged as Zack grabbed one of the umbrellas he'd kept from New York City.

"Fine." Ozzie sighed. "Don't break them."

Zack and Rice opened their doors and hopped out onto the icy steps of city hall. A gust of frigid wind blasted Zack in the face and stung his eyes.

"Zack, look out!" Rice shouted as a rezombified teen-
ager lurched out from behind a stone pillar. He hollered
a kamikaze battle cry and swung the nunchacku at the
frostbitten freak, knocking the undead hooligan flat on
his back. "Dude, did you see that?" Rice asked. "I was like,
Whaa! Come get some! Whaa!" Rice swung the nunchacku
again, emitting a string of kung-fu sound effects.

"Ozzie will be proud." Zack smiled.

When they rounded the back of the truck, Zack saw
that the black iron banister they had crashed into was
half ripped out of the concrete staircase and had hooked
the rear fender, lifting the back wheels a few inches off
the ground.

Zack grabbed the metal bar with both hands and
tugged hard, but it wouldn't budge.

"You need help, Zack?" asked Rice.

"No, I think I can get it," said Zack, hooking
the railing with the umbrella handle. "Just watch
my back."

Rice turned toward the growing horde of

abominable snow zombies. "Ya'll better back up!" he warned.

"Okay, let's give it a try!" Zack shouted up to Ozzie. "On the count of three, hit the gas!"

"One! Two!" With all his strength, Zack yanked back on the umbrella and pried the handrail off the fender. "Three!" The engine roared and the food truck shot down the steps and into the street. The brain-hungry truck vandals flew off the sides of the vehicle and landed splat on the sidewalk.

Down in the street, Zoe threw open the truck's side door and stuck her head out. "Hurry up, dorkbrains! We got cousins to find!"

Zack and Rice sprinted to the truck and hopped in. Ozzie hit the accelerator, and the food truck skidded into motion, spraying up icy slush into the zombie faces behind them.

Want to read the rest of
NOTHING LEFT TO OOZE?

Find out more at www.thezombiechasers.com.

ACKNOWLEDGMENTS

Many thanks to Emilia Rhodes, Rachel Abrams, Sara Shandler, and Josh Bank for all their impeccable zombie-writing advice. And thank you to my fellow New Yorkers for being such great people to zombify.

—J. K.

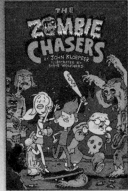
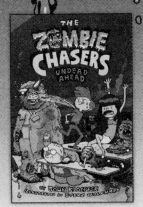